SEXY LIFE, HELLO

"With a masterful balance of tenderness and transgression, care and kink, doubt and power, fear and exposure, Kicherer takes you on a vertiginous journey that will leave you laughing, gasping, blushing and looking over your shoulder."

—Bristol Vaudrin, author of *Afterward*

"Smart, edgy and brimming with wit, Michelle Kicherer's debut novella is a delightful, engrossing ride, leaving the reader wanting more."

—Brooke Totman, *Mad TV, Portlandia*

"…one of the most compelling short reads of the year…a clever examination of purpose, longing and an obscure underside of parasocial sexuality."

—Brianna Wheeler, *Willamette Week*

"An absolute screaming riot of a novella. SEXY LIFE, HELLO is funny and sexy and completely absurd, short and somehow still a full meal."

—Yael van der Wouden, author of Booker Prize finalist, *The Safekeep*

"SEXY LIFE, HELLO is a propulsive novella chocked full of laugh-out-loud moments and exquisite prose as it tells the story of Jane, a former teacher who upon being fired from her teaching job lands two new ones: nanny to twin toddlers and stand-in sexter for a well-known porn star. What ensues is both raunchy hilarity and also a scathing indictment of mass culture's obsessions with celebrity and sex. This is a must-read book!"
—Kerri Schlottman, author of *Tell Me One Thing*

"Jane's teaching career? Over. Her new gig? Simultaneously ghost-sexting for a famous porn star while working as a high-end nanny. Between blending pureed peas and crafting wild fantasies for porn fans, Jane's life is equal parts absurd and thrilling. Her texts get bolder and the boundaries blur, making SEXY LIFE, HELLO a darkly comic exploration of reinvention, fantasy, and the unexpected places we find ourselves when life throws a curveball. Funny and charming and full of heart."
—Achy Obejas, author of PEN/Faulkner finalist, *The Tower of Antilles*

SEXY LIFE, HELLO

A NOVELLA

BY
MICHELLE KICHERER

Banana Pitch Press
Copyright © Michelle Kicherer
All rights reserved
Printed in the United State of America
First Edition: 2024

Library of Congress Cataloging-in-Publication Data
Names: Kicherer, Michelle
Title: Sexy Life, Hello / Michelle Kicherer
Description: First edition. | Banana Pitch Press, 2024
Identifiers: ISBN 979-8-9913071-2-3

Layout design by GRS Editorial, LLC
Cover illustration by Ryan Floyd Johnson

www.bananapitch.com

No part of this publication may be reproduced, distributed, or transmitted in any form or by any means, including photocopying, recording, or other electronic or mechanical methods, without the prior written permission of the publisher, except as permitted by U.S. copyright law.

The story, all names, characters, and incidents portrayed in this production are fictitious. No identification with actual persons (living or deceased), places, buildings, and products is intended or should be inferred.

*For Bronwyn, and any other friend who
keeps the inside jokes flyin*

*And to the Sleuth, who knows the original
"Banana Pitch"*

Elaine: I will never understand people.
Jerry: They're the worst.
                            - *Seinfeld*

The suspense is terrible. I hope it'll last.
            - Gene Wilder (well, Willy Wonka)

SEXY LIFE, HELLO

CHAPTER 1

Note the way she tucks one curl behind her ear but lets the other one dangle, just to the left of her eye. The way she watches, breath catching as the principal makes eye contact. And even though she is almost the same age as Jack, there is still something naughty that comes to mind when she thinks of being sent to his office. The curl falls, she replaces it. They make eye contact. She looks away.

Jack is standing amongst a group of teachers who are griping about so-n-so's behavioral issues or what's-her-face's mom and the budget crises and etcetera and no one seems to like their job besides him. They've all committed, and they're all shackled to their classrooms as if signing up to teach at Verde View Elementary married you to the job, you'd be a bad Catholic for divorcing it.

There's only one male teacher at Verde View, a tall, fifty-something man who teaches fourth grade and gives a lot of thumbs-ups. Otherwise, it's a parade of blondes and brunettes, shiny, straight-haired ladies with thick mascara and voices pitched high. They're all standing in what looks like a hacky sack circle, with Jack somewhere near the middle. He's half a head shorter than all the other teachers but something in his face says he enjoys looking up at them, listening with kind eyes and the nods of someone who will keep their word.

It's hard for her to explain it, but Jane kind of loves Jack's head: he has a short fuzz of hair that fades into shiny baldness that covers his dome like a swim cap. He has a body like a forties weight lifter: his chest is short and expansive, his thighs are thick, his pants sit weirdly high upon his waist over a round belly that looks hard as a pregnant woman's. But soon, Jane will learn, it's not. It's actually soft and luxurious and will make every other man Jane's been with seem juvenile.

He raises his beer, which is served in a plastic cup that says *50 Years!?* They're all drinking from them at a "Happy" Hour event the district coordinates twice a year. Celebrate YOU, the invite always insisted. Everyone groaned.

"Hello, Sweet Jane," Jack says as he walks over to her, and she gets the reference.

"What poppin, Cracker Jack," she says, which is funny to them because when the kids get mad they call him a cracker.

Jack smiles with an expression like he is just the nicest person in the United States of God Blessed America. He likes to say that he puts the "pal" in his title. He says it as a joke but none of the other teachers even smile in its direction. "This June will be the end of your fifth year, huh, Janey? Couple more months?"

"Somehow," Jane says, though she doesn't mean it to sound as cynical as it does. The curl drops from behind her ear and tickles her cheek and she imagines Jack replacing it, cupping her face in his hands.

"We should be living our *lives*!" one of the teachers calls out.

"Seriously!" they moan.

When they look over at Jack he raises his cup that says *50 Years?!* and does what good principals do. He ignores their complaints.

Jane, on the other hand, raises her cup and goes, "Huzzah!" just so she and Jack can watch the other teachers mimic the phrase with confused annoyance on their faces then return to their griping.

"*Eastern*," they'd say. A common refrain. It referred to the trailer park from whence most of the Verde View children came. But even ones who didn't live there would get slapped with the moniker. It'd become a derogatory for any student with behavioral issues, any kid who was hauled in via short yellow bus, arriving at school in time to claim their free breakfast, toss half of said free breakfast into the trash, then mope their way to class.

"Ah, Eastern," Jack would say. "Where little girls dream of being porn stars and little boys dream of watching them." That was a joke they shared, inspired by the fact that one kid's mom *was* a porn star. Used to be. By the time Cameron was in Jane's class, that version of his mom was many versions ago. Most days, by that point, Leah would roll into the parking lot anywhere from twenty minutes to two hours late. Poor Cam would have to wait in Jack's office because no one else was on site except for the custodian by the time she arrived.

Since the start of the school year, Cameron had been having behavioral issues. They'd started off simple—chewing gum, rolling eyes, not turning in homework—but had gotten worse over the school year and now included: flashing other boys, stealing food from kids' lunch boxes, fighting with both boys and girls, and the one that wound up troubling Jane the most: taking so long in the bathroom she swore he was either asleep or had escaped. She half expected one day to bust down the door to see Cameron had slithered down the toilet bowl.

"How often?" Jack asked.

"Every day."

They started having team meetings about what to do, talked with the district psychiatrist, started an Individualized Education Plan.

"Let's continue to check in about Cameron's IEP," said the psychiatrist after reviewing Cameron's home life, his mom's brief history as a porn star, about the guys that'd started coming by the house. "And the nurse says he has impacted feces," she added as she slapped her folder closed then crossed her hands, tilted her head with an expression like, *I know*. "He's afraid to go at home so he holds it in."

Jane sat with that word. *Afraid*. She kept it in mind every time she had to slip Cameron his laxatives at lunch, whisper-promising that none of the other kids are gonna notice, Cam, here take your meds. Sometimes Jane would pour the powdered fiber into his chocolate milk and give the carton a shake, tempting him with the frothy concoction, which he'd gulp to show off his milky brown mustache. Jane would clap to encourage him, her resentment for his mother welling with each slap of her palms.

"Good job, Cam!" she'd say, and that kid would smile so wide it made her sick. "You're doing a good job, bud."

Jane's resentment grew as the months went on. It turned dark and protective on the days when it was her turn to stay with Cameron until his mother arrived. Nearly dusk sometimes, Leah would speed into the classroom in a whirl of twitches, the bleached remnants of her hair flapping at the sides of her thinning face. She'd look at Jane as if her kid's teacher was the asshole for calling again, then bark, "C-*mon*-Cam," all in one snap of a word. "Les' *go*!" And she'd claw for her son's wrist on their way out the door, exchanging it for a cigarette as soon as they crossed the threshold over to Not School.

The same thing happened every few days: "Leah?

Cameron's here waiting for you, can you come pick him up?" Jane would say. "You stupid whorish bitch?" she dreamed of adding. Jane did feel bad for her, though. Everyone had a back story, a reason for being how they were being. Select from the list of why's: alcoholic parent, abusive uncle, foster care, homelessness, or none of the above. Maybe Leah just got waylaid, took a wrong turn or two that weren't reversible. And Jane never liked to use the phrase "bad mother," but if Leah wasn't one? Well.

"I'd *hate* to get CPS involved," Jack would say of all the days he stayed so late, waiting for that rusty Thunderbird to shudder into the parking lot.

"Yeah, no, don't do that," Jane would agree. Jack knew she'd had her own case worker when she was a kid, that she'd grown up just across the way from Eastern, in a little shanty town where the weeds grew around their junk cars, where the yards had no fences and the streets no sidewalks. Coyotes would slaughter hens in the night, cackling after their kill; owls would swoop silently from the trees to pluck feral kittens that dared lope from under their porches. "And you, you'd be out there pissin' by the berry bush," Jack loved to say.

Jane had told him the story of how her family's water got shut off when she was in fourth grade and for nearly a month they all had to go in the backyard. "I happen to like pissin' outside," she'd say, weirdly aroused by the way he'd look at her when he brought it up.

Then one afternoon, Jack called Jane to the principal's office. It was after school, and he did it over the intercom in a tone of feigned seriousness that got her smirking the whole way there. When she appeared in the doorway, Jack perked up at his desk and his eyebrows went up and down like, *Do I have something for you!* Jack opened the top drawer of his desk then made a gesture like, *Close the door!*

Jane closed the door.

Then. There is a moment where things tilt and Jane feels like something is about to happen.

Jack holds up a VHS tape and waggles it around a bit.

"Holy shit," she whispers.

"Ho-lee shit," he agrees.

The tape cover features a blonde woman (Cameron's mom?!) with frizzy '80s bangs and glossy pink lips. She's naked, leaning over a DJ booth at an angle where the vinyl hides the view of her crotch. She's holding up a pair of big puffy headphones that just barely cover her big '80s tits. "She just loves the music," Jack says, pointing at her moaning mouth, at her thin, pursed eyebrows. It was strange to see Leah looking so much younger, her cheeks still fleshy, her lips still full, her hair soft and movable. Vagina still tight and pink, Jane imagines.

While he rolls the science room TV into the middle of his office, finds the extension cord—interjects a joke about budget cuts—Jack tells Jane the story of Cameron's mom. Jane leans on the edge of Jack's desk, arms crossed and listening, happy as if he's just telling her a bedtime story.

One spring day in nineteen eighty-whatever, Leah left Central California for Hollywood. The feeling of packing up your old jalopy with two bags and a dream makes you feel like fire, she was quoted to have said. She would be an actor, pursue the classic dream. But somewhere early on in the mix, she met a guy named Clark Stable who said she had real potential. She starred in a porno that would become infamous, one where she allegedly got pregnant and her co-star, Rock Solid, had allegedly gone bonkers about it, insisting she keep the baby or he'd ruin her career. That's little Rock in there, he was quoted to have said in multiple, televised tangents about how she was supposed to have been "fixed." The papers loved it. "Mass Destruction of Liza Spinelli's Labia"; "Spinelli Ruined After Bestiality Claims"; and an image of Liza Spinelli next to a pig and the headline: "Bankrupt!"

"That one was a tabloid," Jack says. "It looked like someone physically cut up a photo of a pig, glued it next to a photo of Leah, and made copies. *Any*way, after that, no one would hire her—well, no one that wasn't a creepy freak."

"That's really sad," Jane whispers.

"It really is," Jack sighs as he slides the VHS into the slot. "And thus, Liza Spinelli's career was ruined."

"By men," Jane adds. Then the tape whirs to life. They watch Rock Solid sidle up behind Liza Spinelli at her DJ booth, offering something hardly more than a pick up line as he presses her headphones firmly over her ears, holding them there with one hand as his other hand finds the volume on her soundboard. He slides the volume control up. Jane whispers again, "I can't believe that's Cameron's mom."

Jack doesn't respond and suddenly Jane realizes they're watching porn at school. In her head she's like, *Wait, turn this off!* But she's frozen, her arms crossed but also disconnected from her body, each limb is just some fuzzy thing and she doesn't know why the lower limbs don't just take her outta there.

Still. It's captivating. So she says, "Do you think this was the time?"

Jack doesn't say anything and Jane wonders if he's experiencing that fuzzy limb thing, too.

The headphones engulf Liza Spinelli's ears and Rock Solid lifts her skirt, rips her panties in half and enters her. Her face contorts and the people on the dance floor go, *Yeah!* thinking it's just the music she's feeling. Oh god, so good. Liza Spinelli thinks she's on her way to becoming a world famous spinner. Rock Solid pumps to the beat of the music and the crowd is going *Yeah yeah yeah!*

"That's also the name of a character in Final Fantasy," Jack whispers.

"Rock Solid?"

"Liza Spinelli."

They are silent then, aside from the sounds of their swallows, which are very loud, as if even their throats are self-conscious, self-aware. Self, self, focus on yourself. Jane tries not to glance at Jack's crotch (Don't do it!). She's grateful her own erection isn't visible but as soon as she acknowledges it all she can feel is her moistening panties and Rock Solid is biting the soft hair at the back of Liza Spinelli's neck and he's coming inside her and Jack and Jane are breathing and swallowing and she feels creepy as soon as she whispers, "Do you think that was the moment?"

"I dunno, Jane," Jack whispers back as if she'd said something else. And it feels like she has. So when he turns to her, his face is serious and kind and has that same expression he gives the other teachers when he's really and sincerely listening. Like he's a man of his word. Painfully sincere. When his pinky touches the side of Jane's wrist, her body warms. If you touch me, I will come, she wants to whisper, but she can't say anything as her hand finds its way to the hard mound under his pants. Jack gasps in a really quiet way. He takes her wrist as if to stop her but then he doesn't stop her, and then they look at each other's mouths. They aren't breathing. And then, all they're breathing is each other's mouths. It feels as if neither of them have been kissed in a really long time and they're aching and it's so nice that they start crumbling, they can hardly stand.

So, Jane stops standing. She's on her knees, a feeling like tears in her chest as she inhales the scent of Jack's belly. Like coffee and gasoline and tools. This makes her picture him in a trailer park, living in a shanty town, and it makes her love him even though she knows she doesn't love him. It seems to almost pain him as she unzips and she's nearly coming as she rubs her thumb over the dripping head, as she kisses and kisses and it's hardly audible when he murmurs, "Oh, Sweet Jane." She slides him into her mouth and she's closing her eyes and she's so ready to climb up there and sit on the principal's desk, splayed and willing and that's when the custodian walks in.

"The fuck!" the custodian shouts, then, "Back, back!" to someone behind him—Cameron, who, as it turned out, had not been picked up after all.

CHAPTER 2

After getting fired, Jane spent most afternoons sitting on her front porch drinking tequila sunrises and staring into the vacant lot across the street. The house was long-ago obliterated, and the remaining foundation was surrounded by tall brown weeds and remnants of windows glittering purple with sunset. Despite the anxiety surrounding her present life situation, Jane's new afternoon routine was more satisfying than she'd expected. At least, more satisfying than what she'd become used to: lesson planning, waiting for Leah to arrive, serving parking lot duty to adults that forgot the rules of the road as soon as it was time to pick their kids up from school.

She sipped the sunrise, listened to the scurry of nearby varmints.

A couple of weeks went by like that. Once she'd gotten her fill of staring into the void, Jane began applying to the types of jobs that wouldn't check a record. She was, as Jack said with a tone drenched in bitterness, a registered sex offender now. *I'm sorry, Jack,* was the first text she sent after that day. *Miss you, buddy,* was the second. After two weeks of silence, she tried: *You're my dearest friend, Jack.* I have no one, she thought to add as she watched a rat run along the concrete foundation across the street.

Jane only applied for a few jobs: personal assistant for a real estate agent in Pismo Beach, nanny for a couple in Oohlala Beach, and in keeping with her porn theme, sexter for a famous porn star based in Santa Barbara. For that application she'd been a little drunk. In her cover letter she gushed about herself, exaggerating every aspect of her sexuality. Fun! Flirty! Kinky! Wink wink, etcetera!

Too soon? she texted Jack a screenshot of her application. No reply.

She sent a few more applications off. She waited. She watched another rat run across the foundation. It disappeared into the brush, rustled around a while, and then, silence.

*

One week later, Jane parked outside of a three-story house that overlooked Oohlala Beach. It was the kind of home built on the jagged edge of a cliff, the kind that needed thick cement pillars to hold it back from sliding itself into the ocean. Waves and sky and clouds were reflected on its floor-to-ceiling windows like a painting. Gulls ca-cawed as they soared by; pelicans swooped into the ocean below. Tiny people marched along the beach, little flecks of color, voices drowned out by waves. It all made Jane nostalgic for the olden times.

Lorrie and Irene had told her to park in the driveway, but it felt awkward to plant her rust bucket behind their shiny things, so she parked halfway into the ice plant that lined their narrow street. She was five minutes early, so she walked very slowly, up the road, up the drive, and as she got closer, the white noise of ocean started blending with Vivaldi and babies crying and for just a second she was like, Wait, what the hell am I doing?

Before Jane could knock, a security camera on the porch glowed to life. It wasn't the new kind everyone had those days, it was the kind that convenience stores had. Convenience stores from the 90s. Interesting. She smiled at the camera. Imagined Lorrie and Irene watching her from somewhere on the other side, noting her expression, how she carried herself. Jane tried to maintain the posture of an innocent person, a trustworthy person who was not a slutty creep. That's how the Superintendent referred to her when he held out a pale pink notice and gestured toward the door. It's amazing what people will think about you when you tell them you were a teacher. Or, alternatively, if they knew you blew the principal.

*

"Teachers are the real heroes," Irene was saying as she gestured that Jane should sit on one of two sofas that faced each other. "Mimi! Volume down!" she shouted with a double-clap. The Vivaldi quieted and Irene added in a cheeky tone, "We call our sound system Mimi LaRoux. Anyway, sit sit."

Jane sat on the edge of her sofa but wondered if it would be more appropriate that she sit on the floor with the ten-month old twins, Franny and Zooey. They were at that perfect baby age where they couldn't talk yet but they could sit upright on their own. Between them was a picnic basket full of wooden fruit. Franny, or Zooey, took out a wooden banana and shook it around before throwing it a few feet and smiling as if that was a funny thing she'd done. Jane wanted to ask what other activities the babies were fond of besides chucking fruit but she didn't want to make it seem like she'd never been around babies before, which was the truth. So she simply smiled and nodded at Zooey, or Franny, as if she'd done a good thing by throwing that banana.

"So!" Irene said as she leaned toward the steaming mug that sat on the round wooden coffee table between them. She dunked her tea bag slowly, once, twice, then set it on a little plate in the shape of a heart. She leaned further forward, then, sipping from the mug without picking it up. Her slick, chin-length hair slipped from behind her ears and stuck to the corners of her lips. When she sat upright again the hair was still there. It was as if she had food stuck to her mouth and Jane wanted to tell her that she had a little something.

"But she wants to be a writer!" Lorrie called from the kitchen, where she was making Jane an espresso from a machine that pumped out foamy little drinks using silver pods with flavors like Sanctimonious and Everglade. Jane had selected a flavor called Glorious. The machine was sputtering gloriousness into a cup as Lorrie called, "Cream, you said!"

"Yes, please!" Jane called back. She forgot that in her cover letter she had said something about being an aspiring writer, only because the ad mentioned how both women worked in the literary field. Why had she written that? She didn't like writing. She didn't even like reading.

"Well anyhow, I appreciate your service," Irene added in a tone that was hard to decipher. She leaned toward her tea cup again and made that sipping face people make when their drink is quite hot but very tasty.

"Oh, well, thank you," Jane said with a tone meant to say: I don't *deserve* this kinda praise.

Irene smiled. Jane smiled. Both women sat on the edge of their sofas.

"So, this is the abode," Irene said, waving her hands as if to say, this ol' dump. Their house looked like something that would be featured in *Architectural Digest*. The walls were painted in delicately varied tones of gray. When Jane looked down at the multicolored tiles under her feet, Irene said, "Those are imported from Morocco," and when Jane noticed the only cheesy thing on the wall—a clock in the shape of a train—Irene said, "Gift from granddad. It choo-choos on the hour."

"I *hate* that thing!" Lorrie was saying as she entered the room with an orange espresso cup and saucer set in each hand. "But if we took it down, my dad would look for it every time he came over. Here's your Glorious."

Jane didn't know how seriously Lorrie took the naming of her espresso flavors so she simply smiled and thanked her and tipped back the whole thing in one go, not realizing how little was actually in her cup. The wild rush of caffeine made it difficult to focus her eyes for a second and Jane imagined them talking about her after she left. Did you *see* that? Think she takes her liquor like she takes her espresso?

Jane smiled at Lorrie, who smiled back from where she sat cross legged on the floor with Franny and Zooey. Aside from baby coos and the sound of wooden fruit clacking against each other, no one was saying anything. So Jane smiled again, trying to maintain an expression that looked easygoing. She was trying so hard to seem nice that she felt nefarious, like the second one of them looked away she'd pry a Moroccan tile from the floor and slip it into her purse.

The fruit chucking baby pulled a bunch of wooden grapes from the basket and ran her tiny fingers along the bumpy purple outlines. Her sister was trying to fit a wooden apple into the front pocket of her overalls.

"I love their fruit collection," Jane said.

"Great, huh? My sister sent these from Belgium," Lorrie said as she got up to retrieve the banana. She pretended to talk on the banana phone as she said, "Well, so you want to be a writer. Is that right?" She handed the banana to Franny, or Zooey, and looked at Jane with an expression that urged: *Do tell*.

"Oh, yes," Jane said, nearly believing herself when she went, "I've always wanted to be a writer, but never earnestly pursued it."

Irene looked at Lorrie as if to say: *If I had a nickel*.

That was Jane's cue to add: "The time is now."

Nods of approval. The wooden banana flew across the room.

"Precisely right," Lorrie said. The couple went on to explain their respective roles. Lorrie ran a literary organization that sponsored events throughout the Central Coast. Irene was a famous writer of shitty mystery novels. When Irene said who she was, Jane mentioned the many places she'd seen her books: airports, bookstore windows, Target. Jane smiled politely as she thought about how ridiculous it was that millions of people around the world were reading Irene's garbage. But it made sense; a lot of people are idiots.

"*Good* for you for changing jobs at this point in your life," Lorrie said.

Jane nodded as if this were some sacrifice she'd made. "Thirty-two seems old to shift careers. But, it also feels like the *right* time," Jane said, referencing how she could write during the girls' naptime. "*If* that's okay with you."

Nods of approval, hand waves like, of *course*.

"You know, a *lot* of people stay stuck in jobs because it's easier," Lorrie agreed, accompanying her statement with a gesture meant to demonstrate her mind was blown by this mistake.

"Certainly," Irene chimed in. "People are too scared to try something else."

Lorrie nodded. Jane nodded.

"Complacency is a sin," Lorrie said as if she were reciting a commandment.

The women repeated a different version of that same sentiment when they called hours later and offered Jane the job. The twins will be delighted to have you, they'd said of the girls, who seemed easy enough, as far as babies go. Lorrie and Irene asked if Jane would be able to start the following Monday, which was the first of May.

"May Day," Jane said, looking at the calendar.

"May Day," the women agreed, and it seemed clear that none of them remembered what that meant. And then there was a pause, in which Jane thought they were going to ask something else. A contingency, a hired-after-your-reference-check moment. She was glad they couldn't see her expression during this pause, where her heart was skipping over beats and she waited for the part where they'd ask why she didn't at least finish out the school year. But they didn't ask. And it felt clear, as they said goodbye, see you Monday, that Lorrie and Irene trusted Jane. That Jane seemed like a good person. And she was, really. She was.

CHAPTER 3

It didn't take long for Jane to get acquainted with Lorrie and Irene's house. The girls' room with its own little balcony; Lorrie and Irene's room with its jacuzzi tub in the bathroom; and most spectacularly, and a room they called The Library: a dark green room with bookshelves that required one of those rolling ladders like in *Beauty and the Beast*. The shelves were lined mostly with mystery novels. The desk was covered in teal sticky notes and multicolored pens.

"That's how Irene brainstorms," Lorrie explained.

Teetotaler, one note said.

Hobnob.

Chin hairs.

By the second week, Jane and the girls had gotten into a pretty good routine. After breakfast she'd stroll them along the boardwalk in their two-baby stroller, hoping no one thought they were hers. Once they got back she'd ease their warm, sleepy bodies into their cribs and as soon as the crying faded to whimpers and finally, sweet silence, she'd take the baby monitor out onto the sundeck overlooking Oohlala Beach. Sometimes she'd read but usually she'd just fall asleep on the lounge chair, the sounds of waves and distant voices lulling her away. Some days it felt good to doze out there, and others, she'd jolt awake feeling pathetic and restless.

One afternoon while lounging in the sun, Jane perused the online classifieds. She wasn't looking for anything, really, but the job descriptions themselves provided interesting fodder. In the Writing Gigs section, she'd see things like:

Scan and Catalog Antiquarian Books
Literary Assistant for Amish Writer
Storytelling Eulogizer for End of Life Celebrations

She wondered if she shouldn't have accepted the first job she was offered. What was she doing out there with her precious life, pushing babies down a beach? What was she *supposed* to be doing? And, as if some force from the beyond answered her curiosity, a new email popped up. The subject read, *Re: writing for me! xo - Lola*

Immediately, she jotted a text: *Jack! I got an interview request from that porn star who wants someone to sext for her!* Jane stared at the text until it reported *Delivered*. She waited for some indication he was reading it, typing his reply. She imagined that Jack was turned on by this job prospect of hers, that it'd help him to snap out of his own job-loss daze. He'd support her new endeavor and would even help her think of great lines. Sometimes, she'd sext while they boned, using their own bodies as inspiration. They'd think of Liza Spinelli, how she keeps her headphones on as Rock Solid goes at her from behind. And Jack's scent, she'd take it in. Wafts like coffee and gasoline. Jack and Jane are breathing each other, and he doesn't look away from her face as he enters her, because he loves her and they love this.

What are you doing, job-wise? she added after a few minutes. Maybe she was coming on too strong. Or maybe she wasn't being sincere enough. People had told her that before. Practice sincerity, she'd read on a tea bag. *I'm sorry all of this happened,* she typed, then deleted. She imagined Jack sitting at home, half awake and dribbling coffee down his chin. He'd fall asleep on the couch by five, wake at midnight to snack, return to his bed restless for productivity but too depressed to do anything. Jack had loved being a principal. What would he do now?

The look on Jack's face right before Jane's lips touched his lips said something like, I can't believe I get to kiss you. She imagines him thinking that, thinking of her now and later and all the time. Maybe he was seeing her texts but was too wrecked to respond. A man, ruined. Jane's tongue swirls the tip, she closes her eyes.

I like your vibe! Lola's email began. It broke down the base rate and the commissions, how often she'd get paid.

It seemed as though this could be quite the lucrative arrangement. Jane searched *What is a professional sexter?* Then: *What is a ghost sexter?* A bunch of articles popped up about how much money you could make. It was more than she'd ever be able to make as a teacher. What the?

So much she could do with that kind of money. Move away, buy a house, get… something. And then Jane's screen got tired of waiting for her to return her internet wandering and flicked to black. A shadowy glass figure reflected back at her with a frown that rolled the chin down like it was dough being pinned; the eyes glared over gray pockets; the outline of curl was somehow both frizzy and flat.

The ad promised that looks didn't matter, you'd never have to actually speak and no one would ever see your face. Sexting only. Just kinky, fun, and flirty.

Jane woke her screen again. Stared at Lola's email. Reread it, twice.

Complacency is a sin.

Great! Jane was typing, and, *So looking forward to meeting you, Lola!* She thought of those girls in the late night commercials, asking if you wanted a friend. On the television they were sexy blondes, gently biting the tips of their fingers and looking into the camera with sleepy, seductive eyes. Those chicks couldn't actually be the voices on the phone when lonely men called. Jane imagined the real women on the line, describing what they'd do to you and on you and for you. They were probably pudgy and pockmarked, they had lazy eyes and messy hair. They respectfully put their hands over the receiver when they took a bite of pizza, they turned the volume down on their phones while the men masturbated, they went home to cats and drafty homes and loneliness. They were like her.

*

The last time Jane went on a date was several months before. Some guy named Dave from an app called Finder! She'd planned on making a joke about the name when she arrived. Something like how she could have used it the last time she lost her keys. Or, something funny, she mused as she pulled up in front of a dive called Slappy's. When Jane arrived five minutes early, Dave was already sitting at the bar, half a skunky beer in his hand. Jane was wearing heels that sounded plasticky and cheap and when she clacked up to the bar, and Dave turned around with a smile at the ready. All it took for her to never see him again was the flickering dim of that smile, then its replacement with another, faker smile that did not mask his disappointment.

That's how Jane felt as she waited for Lola to show up for their virtual interview. Like Lola's camera would turn on and she'd have that same kinda look Dave had, like when you dribble something down your chin and hope no one notices before you wipe it away.

Two minutes late! See you soon! Lola's message said.
No worries! Jane replied, though she was worried.

They'd set up a time to chat when Jane knew Franny and Zooey would be napping. She parked herself in their kitchen, careful to show the view of the beach in the background, to get her tiny orange espresso cup in view of the camera. She picked it up by its clumsy little handle and took a sip. Euphoria, the flavor was called. She took another sip and felt no such thing.

For the interview, Jane had tied her hair into a big curly bun and wore dangly silver earrings that made her think of a fortune teller. She applied a thick coat of peachy lipstick. A drop of sweat rolled down her side.

At the hour, she clicked the link Lola had sent her. For two painful minutes she watched herself on camera as she waited. She parted her lips and tugged a curl loose from her bun so that it hung seductively along the side of her face. She was wearing a mid-length skirt, which she hiked a little higher up her thighs, though her camera only showed her top half. What if Lola asked her to stand up? To do a little twirl, and show what her momma gave her? Do looks really not matter?

Part of the application process included a questionnaire. One of the questions said:

Convince me to buy a three minute custom video of you (AKA: me) jerking off a plastic sheep while talking about your love of wool sweaters. In a conversational, message-y way, not a newspaper ad sorta way.

Jane's answer was:

Hey babe, what're you up to? I'm wearing this super soft cashmere sweater and it gave me this idea. It's kinda dirty tho. I wanna praise sheep for being so good at making wool… but I also wanna fuck sheep. Confusing, right? So I have my favorite plastic one here…. If I do something kinda kinky with him, will you watch?

Jane tried to imagine herself in such a scenario, trying to turn someone on from afar as she took on the persona of a woman fake-fucking a plastic sheep. How would she feel if she actually got the job? She tried to imagine herself sitting crossed-legged on the floor, scrolling through video content for the perfect clip of Lola jerking off plastic sheep while whispering sweet nothings into its plastic ears. How many videos and pictures of Lola naked or fucking things would Jane have to see?

Then, a black screen appeared. Lola's camera and mic were both off, but the video app said that Caller had entered the room. Jane's first reaction was that she'd been tricked. There was no Lola on the other end of that computer. Maybe Lola never existed. It was probably some fat old dude who set up these "interviews" to get off; he just wanted to see what types of chicks would apply to be sexters on behalf of a porn star. He would get to see the women on the other side of the late night commercials. They weren't blonds. They were frizzy-headed chubby chicks who ate pizza and lazily responded to the men on the line. They'd call all their clients sweetie or honey or baby and congratulate them when they came. Jane pressed a tuft of her curl behind her ear, thought of Dave's expression, how poorly he hid his disappointment when he saw what Jane looked like in person.

And then a voice spoke. It sounded like Drew Barrymore. "Hey, sorry! Hold on *one* sec." The screen remained black while Caller made rustling sounds like she was just settling in.

Jane smiled shyly, looking into the glowing green light that indicated her own camera was on. Her own face was in the upper right corner of the screen. She tried not to look at it, and she tried not to think about Dave's feigned smile and instead, surprisingly, she thought of the look on Jack's face, right before they kissed.

And then, she appeared. Lola. She was sitting cross-legged on a bed wearing baggy gray sweats and a loose gray sweatshirt that hung off one shoulder. Her hair was blonde, as expected, but it was ratty and pulled to one side like an '80s workout instructor. Lola wore no makeup. She even had gray under her eyes. Like me! Jane thought.

"Sorry, *one* sec," Lola said again, holding up a finger.

Her nails were long and pink and somehow both soothing and annoying when she clacked them on the keys. She was sitting on a plush-looking bed, half a dozen velour pillows arranged neatly along the tufted cloth headboard behind her. Jane imagined Lola filming scenes on that bed. An imaginary hand would push her onto her back, she'd look back at the camera with a face like, come-n-get-me.

"Okay *anyway*," Lola said with a face like, You know how it is.

Jane gestured like, *Oh do I ever*.

"Okay, so first off, I *loved* your storytelling in your questionnaire. That one about being codfish together, swimming into the darkest crevices of the ocean?"

"The one where I said, 'be my cock fish?'"

"YES!" Lola snapped her fingers and clapped once. She smiled widely. What tiny teeth she had!

"Does that kind of thing come up a lot?" Jane asked as she touched one of her dangly earrings, wishing she could slip them off. She thought of the phrase *mutton dressed as lamb*. When Lola tilted her head, Jane clarified, "I mean, pretending to be animals?"

"Oh my god, yes. *All* the time," Lola said. She clapped her palms together so that her shiny pink nails splayed in the shape of a V. She raised her eyebrows up and down then winked. "It's kind of my *brand*. Kinda kooky, you know? How do you *feel* about that?"

"I *love* it!" Jane found herself saying, mimicking Lola's

clap. "I'm a writer, so storytelling is part of what gets me off," she said, borrowing from her other lie. It was so surprising. But so easy. "Who doesn't love to pretend to be a kinky animal?" she added.

"*Right?* Okay, that's great. *So* great. Oh *thank* you, Marielle," Lola added to someone off camera. Lola's hand reached out of view and returned holding a green smoothie in a tall glass, like the kind used for old-timey milkshakes. She took a long sip from the straw then rimmed the tip of her tongue around her lips. "*MMM.* Divine." Lola peered into the camera, then. Her eyes glowed with something sweet and devious and exciting and it was easy to see why men would want to stare into those very eyes as they whacked off.

Jane recalled one part from the questionnaire:

You're tired, not in the mood for bullshit. And of course that's when one of your regulars signs on and starts calling you names, because that's how he gets off. He's turned his camera on and he's very slowly massaging his penis, very close to the camera, saying he's very mad at you. He's making demands and saying, "What're you gonna do to make me feel better?"

Would that happen?

Lola took a sip of her smoothie and laid sideways on her bed like they were just a couple of gals having pillow talk. While one hand propped her head up, the other undid her hair and a cascade of blonde spread down her shoulders, her arm. Jane knew what was coming next. She tried to think of her best sexual anecdote, quickly quickly, but all she could think of was her most recent sexcapade. That's what she'd called it when Lola asked. A sexcapade, as if that's how she always referred to her sexual encounters, as if they were so frequent and so wild they had to be named. She'd describe the oddly arousing scent of his stomach, his face—earnest and sad—and the hardening under his pants, the way he almost said *No no no!* How he'd gestured to *Close the door* but had actually meant *Lock it*. But that's what made it exciting for Jane, how any moment someone could walk in. Oh, the hurried frenzy of it! Eyes darting to the door, eyes closed, eyes open, mouths on necks and lips on cock and eyes now closed and—

"You know?" Lola said and Jane was like, *Shit, wait, what?*

"Yeah," Jane said, sounding all dreamy. And luckily, Lola kept talking.

"It was for these ugly bras with no underwire. They're meant for moms or something. I think they were *exclusively* sold at JCPenney."

"I used to want to be a model, too," Jane said, wiping the sexcapade from her mouth.

"It's not always glamorous but it's a toe-in, sometimes. You know?"

"Yeah, like a shoe-in," Jane said.

Lola looked at her blankly like, Uhm, what?

Then Jane blurted out: "I got caught shoplifting there when I was younger."

"Oh *god*, yeah. I mean, I still steal sometimes. Just for fun." Lola winked and sat up, ran her fingers through her hair, then lay on her back. Jane got nervous, again, preparing herself for talking about sex. Maybe Lola would start fingering herself, just to see what Jane would do. Maybe she'd stare into Jane's eyes, rimming her lips with her tongue again and she'd moan into the camera until her eyes closed in ecstasy. But she just kept talking about JCPenney and what she referred to as mom-bra modeling. "So yeah, I was doing that a few years, then I was bartending at this place called Twinkies." She leaned up to look directly at the camera. "You know Twinkies?"

"No," Jane confessed.

"I was never one of the dancers there," she said a bit brusquely, as if it might be rude to assume so. Lola sat up again, set her smoothie down out of view. She wrapped her arms around her knees. It was both hard and easy to imagine her sitting in that same posture naked. What must it feel like to be so comfortable in your body? Lola smacked her tongue against her teeth and jumped into specifics as if they'd been over them many times. She seemed to start mid-conversation, as if Jane had heard most of it before. "So, yeah. You'll be sexting with multiple people at a time and you just kinda pick up from where the last staffer left off. They hand it over to you."

"Right," Jane said as if she was familiar.

But Lola was well-versed in tone reading and further explained, "Think of it like, you're at a party passing a phone around to a friend and you're all texting the same guy. So, when one person passes the phone to you, you can see the rest of the convo and just keep going."

Jane had never been to a party where that would have happened but she nodded and gestured with a face like: That makes sense!

"And yeah, obviously there's always gonna be one guy who wants to be a baby, or he wants you to be a gerbil that'll crawl into his butt and nibble away the poo so you can fit inside his rectum and live there. Lotta classic scat fantasies." Lola waved a hand like, *Whatever!*

Jane also waved a hand like, whatever. And just then, she heard what sounded like Zooey crying from the other room. When she'd shared with Lorrie and Irene that she could already tell the twins' cries apart, they were impressed. When Jane added that she could also tell the scent of their poops apart, they seemed weirded out.

"Sorry," Jane said, looking over her shoulder toward the girls' room.

"No *worries!* Mine are in the other room right now," Lola said, adding, "Content, I hope," with a look like: *You know kids.*

Jane felt stupid for assuming someone like Lola wouldn't have kids. "*Oh* yeah," she said, unsure why she stopped herself from saying she was just the nanny.

"How old?" Lola asked, picking up her smoothie again, bringing the straw between her lips and not sucking. She seemed pleased by their new bond of motherhood. When Jane said they just turned eleven months, Lola gasped, "*Twins*! That's so beautiful! Mine are two and four. And I mean, time just *flies*, doesn't it?"

Jane couldn't think of what else to say, so she tilted her head in a way meant to indicate she was watching time pass.

Lola held up a finger and said, "Well, just a couple quick logistics before you go."

Jane tried to ignore the term "logistics" and smiled, took notes. Zooey wailed in the background and Jane jotted faster, as if that'd get Lola to speak more quickly.

"Any questions?" Lola asked.

Jane glanced at her notes: four-hour shifts, importance of responding to people right away, all the messaging done through an app. "I can download the app on my phone?" was her only question.

"No no no, you have to use a computer for the messaging, since it's eighteen and over content." Lola waved a hand as if to say, *Obviously*.

Jane imagined having her laptop out while she nannied, sexting about gerbils in butts while the babies cooed and played with their wooden fruit.

"Your goal is to get the clients to want to see exclusive content," Lola was saying, rubbing her fingers together to signify money. "The tips can be good if you play 'em right. Then it's like, they're putting hypothetical bills down your hypothetical G string."

At that, Jane blushed, for some reason imagining Lola slipping dollar bills into her skirt. Then the skirt would be undone and Jane would be stepping out of it. Lola's long nails would graze Jane's skin as Lola arranged the bills around the hem of Jane's panties. Jane would twist her hips around like a hula dancer in her big, thick money skirt. In this fantasy, Jane's skin was as smooth and taut as Lola's skin and she was thin, her hip bones jutting out like handles.

Just then Franny started crying, too, and Jane felt lame when she declared, "Two sets of lungs are definitely louder than one!"

But Lola was a pro. She was used to making people feel relaxed. She didn't just smile in response, she glowed. "Sweeties," she said, hand to her heart, blowing a kiss in the direction of the girls. And though the word *phony* came to mind, Jane couldn't help but feel comforted when Lola clasped both of her hands to her heart, as if holding their two hearts together between her breasts. The gesture made Jane want to crawl through the camera and onto Lola's big, plush bed. They'd snuggle up under the covers of her golden velour duvet, they'd sink down into all of her regal throw pillows, and Lola would show Jane exactly what she gave the men on camera.

Lola was putting her hair into another ponytail and crossing her arms like she was hugging herself and Franny and Zooey were crying and Jane was waiting. Waiting for Lola to whisper something more. One of the questions on the application asked: *What was your kinkiest sexual encounter?* Jane wrote about Jack and Liza Spinelli, elaborating on the way she swirled her tongue around his tip, how she loved the taste, how she wanted to suck his dick like a—

"Well, I'll let you go, sweetie!" Lola cooed.

And Jane went, "Yay!"

Lola blew a kiss goodbye and Jane caught it, feeling both foolish and sexy as she planted it on her own cheek. By the time she thought to kiss her fingertips and blow one back, the screen went dark and Lola was gone and all Jane could hear was the sound of two babies crying.

CHAPTER 4

That afternoon Jane snuggled on the couch with Franny and Zooey, watching a show called *Sparkle Baby*, in which several babies sat around in a sparkly purple room banging toys together and cooing and crying. She wanted to tell Jack about her interview with Lola, but when she reached for her phone, a text awaited.

Super nice to meet you today :)

For the rest of *Sparkle Baby*, Jane thought about how to respond. She pictured herself lying on her back on a big plush bed, sending sexts to guys all over the world. Probably some ladies, too. Maybe they'd chat and they'd pay Jane to keep them company, or maybe they'd go right into it. *Show me your pussy! Show me your asshole! Put a gerbil up your butt!*

Finally, Jane wrote: *Same, so nice!*

A yellow lab puppy waddles into the *Sparkle Baby* room. All but one of the babies gravitate towards it. The last baby, who is holding what looks like two purple drum sticks made of papier-mâché, starts crying. There's an obvious edit in the scene, then the crying baby is no longer in the room.

While Franny and Zooey watched the sparkly, baby-filled room with glazed eyes, Jane searched stuff like *Lola* and *mom-bra model* and *sexting* and *Twinkies*. She was not disappointed in what she found.

*

The next afternoon Jane sat in a big plush chair at Curlicue, a salon in San Luis Obispo that exclusively did curly haircuts. It was owned by a woman named Carrie, who mostly went by Curly, and who had become one of Jane's closest friends. Jane showed Curly the email she'd gotten that morning. The subject read: *Yay!*

"You're hired, baby!" Curly read aloud, pointing her scissors at the speech bubble next to a picture of Lola in a cheerleader outfit, licking a V sign she was making with her fingers. "Damn, those titties are just waiting to bust out of that top."

"Judge not lest ye be judged, *Curly*."

"I'm not *judging*, I'm just…*saying*."

"Right. Well check this out." Jane scrolled through an attachment called "How to Engage Your Sexters." It detailed things like: *How to login to Lola's messaging account, When to send pictures and videos, How to prompt clients to tip.*

"I'm surprised at her efficiency," Curly was saying as she trimmed a renegade curl on the side of Jane's face.

"Yeah, I guess she has a few sexters working for her.

I mean, she has, like, millions of followers. She's, like, a mega millionaire. Can you make these curls kinda frame my face?"

"I seriously can't believe you're doing this," Curly said, picking up a curl and carefully snipping off a quarter inch. She placed it next to Jane's eye and tilted her head, then snipped a little more. "I thought this was just a joke?"

"I thought you'd be more impressed," Jane said, looking at the tattoo of a naked, joint-smoking witch that straddled Curly's thigh. Curly's hair was cut into a thick curly mohawk, a 'do she kept telling Jane would look great on her. It's slimming, she'd insist when Jane sighed about her doubling chin.

"I mean, I *am* impressed," Curly said, picking up a new curl, snipping it, then setting it down. "But. I have a hard time imagining you sitting there having phone sex all day. What about the kids? I mean, are you gonna quit the nanny thing?"

Jane explained that the shifts overlapped with when she nannied. She shrugged. "Two birds with one stone."

"So you're going to be sending sexts about cock 'n balls while you're giving babies their bottles?"

"More like, tits 'n ass. Anyway, I'm just *curious*." Jane said. "Judgy."

"Oh, shush." Curly focused on a curl, held it up, squinted. Snip snip. "You love porn stars. Remember that guy you dated?"

"You mean hated?" Jane said, because she knew exactly what Curly was about to say. "And he wasn't a porn star. He was a photographer."

"Specializing in underwater nude photography," Curly said, like she was quoting from his website.

"Aaaand then he left me for a stripper."

"He was so cliché," Curly agreed. "Remember that line he said?"

They recited it together: "'If there are two things I'm confident in, it's my work, and my dick.'"

"He did have a huge dick. But he was awful in bed, so who cares," Jane said.

"You know, I've always wanted to know what it'd be like to get pummeled by a thing like that." Curly set her scissors down and measured to show how long. "Like a big cucumber."

"My pussy could hardly accommodate it."

"Alright, so, you do you have good material. Just say stuff like that. When do you start again?"

"Tomorrow."

"Holy shit," Curly said, then she stopped and pointed at Jane with her scissors. "Wait. You have a face like you're thinking of something."

Curly was standing behind Jane in the salon chair. They looked at each other in the mirror. She put her hands over Jane's eyes.

"I'm not," Jane said.

"Yes you are." Curly made an opening in her fingers so Jane could peek through them. "You're thinking about Jack."

"I'm not!" she lied. But as soon as Curly wasn't looking, Jane checked her phone again. But of course, he still hadn't responded.

CHAPTER 5

Jane's first afternoon on the Lola job started while the girls were eating lunch. She'd just read through the note Irene had left, which instructed her how to thaw four cubes of frozen puréed peas by placing them in a saucepan on low heat. Same for the little frozen cubes of puréed blueberries, apples and carrots. Every day so far, Irene left a note for Jane that was almost identical to the one before it:

1. Defrost the frozen breast milk in a bowl of warm water, never microwave
2. Let the girls take their time eating
3. Let them hold their spoons if they want
4. Let them get messy!
5. If they're not hungry, don't force it
6. Have a smart and happy day!

"Good girl," Jane was saying to Franny. Like she was a dog. "Good girl!" she added as Zooey took a bite. Jane's computer was propped on the kitchen table. At 11:59 she signed into Lola's account. Immediately a message came through. *Hey lover. What are you doing?* Lola's training materials had suggested you match their language and tone. The guy's screen name was DonaldMuck. Jane spooned a big bite of puréed carrot into Zooey's mouth and wrote, *Hey lovey. You caught me in a messy moment.*

I want to see, he wrote, clicking the button for Premium Photo.

Jane mused, *What if I just sent him a picture of two messy babies, their faces splattered with multicolored mush?* Instead, she sent a close-up of Lola's wet pussy.

It went on from there. While some customers wanted to get right into the sexy stuff, some just wanted to talk. Lola had warned about that, saying that there's a fine line between gaining their trust and just entertaining them for free. *You're not there to be their buddy*, the training manual reminded. *You're there to get them to tip.* She stressed that if a customer wasn't tipping within twenty minutes, to get a little pushier. *Get them to wanna see more ;) Sometimes you'll have to act like their friend, sometimes you'll have to come off like you want to get to know them. But as soon as possible, make it seem like you want them. Get them to buy more and more and more premium content.*

What are you wearing? was the opening line from a guy named StarShootsShot.

Jane looked down at her jeans, the little splatter of blueberry purée on her knee. Her pale green t-shirt had a big wet circle in the middle from where she'd spilled breast milk on herself then scrubbed it with too much soapy water.

I'm actually not wearing anything. Teehee! she wrote. *My breasts are dripping hot.* Had anyone ever described their breasts in such a way? But before she could even feel stupid, the reply said: *Show me.* Jane scrolled through Lola's photo library to see if there was anything that might signify hot and dripping breasts. She found one where Lola is ripping off a bright red fishnet bodysuit in the shower. *Can you imagine how wet I am, babe?*

You are so incredible, Lola.

Zooey started sniffling then and Jane went, "Oh hi Zo-Zo, you ready for a nap?" Then Jane was picking up one now-crying baby, then the other, laying them down on the changing table one at a time. Whisper-singing as she changed one baby, then the other. At one point, Jane told Curly, *I can't believe how natural it was.* To feed the babies, change them.

You're a natural, Curly had said. Jane thought of that as she put the girls down for their naps. As she hummed them to sleep. As she shut the door and opened her laptop.

There are two things I'm confident in, she wrote. *My pussy, and this outfit.* She sent over a picture of Lola with her hand traveling down the front of that same ripped body suit. Her pinky is tangled in the netting and her lip is curled as if she can't wait to untangle that little pinky and stick it in her pinky. Jane considered saying something like that but it seemed too stupid.

And yet.

When StarShootsShot asked to know what Lola was doing in that picture, that's exactly what Jane wrote. *Pinky in the pinky, maybe one in the stinky.*

I love it, wrote StarShootsShot. *I am so hard.* He pressed the button for Premium Video.

Let me make you the perfect video, baby, Jane typed to buy some time. She rinsed out bowls of blueberry mush, hand washed the girls' bottles, and sent over a ten-second clip of Lola fingering herself in the red fishnet. By the time she plopped down on the couch Jane had chatted with four different customers and made over a hundred dollars in commissions.

Yeah? Well now you're making *me* hard, she replied to another guy. They loved telling her how hard they were. What else is new, she imagined writing. Jane took a bite of pizza and licked the sauce from the corner of her mouth. Just like the late night girls, she mused. The real girls, the behind-the-scenes ones. She wanted to tell Jack about all the scenes she was setting up for those guys, the funny ways in which she'd describe herself getting hard or getting wet. Dripping wet, spraying wetness down her legs. She laughed as she sent over a picture of Lola with a finger up her butt.

The commissions ticked higher.

By the time Irene and Lorrie got home, Jane's sexting shift had ended and she'd made nearly three hundred dollars in commissions. It was so easy. It was so stupid. And as she was saying 'bye to the girls and their moms, Jane got a text from Lola.

Wow, what did you do!? it said, which at first was startling. Then she sent a kissy cartoon cat face and congratulated Jane on a huge first day in sales. *You, my lady, are a star.*

Jane replied with the 😌 emoji.

She tiptoed down the steps and toward her car, a shitty old Corolla with rusty hubcaps and a bumper sticker that said, *Take a picture, it'll last longer*. It was cool and breezy out for May but still, she rolled down the windows, captured handfuls of air as she drove along the road next to Oohlala Beach. The world was looking oysterlike. She squinted up toward the sun, feeling just like that, like fire.

CHAPTER 6

The first few days as Lola's sexter went much the same. While Jane did her best to not picture any of the men on the line, she soon realized that the photo and video sharing component was more a part of the deal than she'd anticipated. These folks didn't want to just see videos of Lola touching herself or humping a stuffed dog. And yes, sometimes they just wanted to talk (*Hey! How's your day? How ya doin'?*). But often, they wanted to share their sexual expertise as well. So while Jane was over there defrosting bags of breast milk, she was answering men who'd sent videos of themselves masturbating into a bowl of Cheerios then eating it, or painfully, it seemed, butt-fucking themselves with various objects. There were classics like shower-mounted dildos or cucumbers; and there were more creative things like writing utensils and dog toys, shoe horns and Barbies. A lot of action figures went into buttholes.

Jane tried not to watch their faces, glancing at the videos just long enough to get the gist of what they were doing so she could respond appropriately. To help her get through some of the more absurd moments, Jane imagined these men were just joking, that afterwards the guy would jump up and laugh, wave a hand like, *Oh god, so stupid, right?*

There was also a different variety of customer that Jane wasn't expecting. These were the ones who wanted to hear grotesque fantasies. Jane had come to think of this category as *mystical bestiality*, wherein the men would dream up creative ways to fuck a cyclops-dragon or a satyr. There was a creature called the Typhon, which she'd learned about from a client named MonsterCming. He explained that the Typhon was the "father of all monsters." *Daddy issues?* Jane wanted to type, but instead, she'd described the hideous serpentine creature in sensual detail: his bat wings and double fangs, his shoulders covered in snakes. The snakes were always biting MonsterCming while also penetrating him, threatening to cut him or strangle him. MonsterCming's body would teeter between fear and pleasure for sometimes upwards of two hours. Every time his screen name popped up, Jane had to mentally prepare for all the mystical role-playing ahead. But freaky dudes like MonsterCming were the best tippers, and often were very respectful and sweet in a way that was surprising.

Scat was another popular obsession. These boys wanted Lola to shit her pants then reach down there and dig around, wash herself in her own feces. Jane would go, *Yes, daddy, I did poop my pants*, and they'd say she was a bad girl and needed a bath. So Jane would tell *them* that she wanted to just bathe in her own feces, then get rinsed clean by a golden shower. They'd delight to piss all over her, harnessing a strong stream of urine through their raging boners.

Cha-ching.

Go ahead and douse me in pee pee, papi. Jane pictured herself on a bed, not getting pissed on but lying on her back, tossing handfuls of cash into the air. When they cried, *I'm shitting on your face!* She'd go *YES!!!! Cha-chingy-ching-ching!* Jane imagined marching into a bank, dropping armfuls of cash money on a teller's counter. The teller would cock their head like, *Where'd it come from?* And Jane would say, *Pee pee poo poo*, and they'd know exactly what she meant.

Throughout these interactions, Jane was spooning mouthfuls of mushed carrots and puréed broccoli into Franny and Zooey's hungry mouths. The contrast in content versus real life might have been more disturbing if she wasn't so consistently busy with both activities. Sometimes, she'd have her laptop out during mealtimes or reading, or she'd jot quick responses between diaper changes and bottle feeding. But usually, her sexting shift didn't interfere with much of the day; she'd planned it perfectly to start right around lunch time and extend through the girls' two-to-three-hour afternoon nap. *They're great sleepers*, Irene had cooed in their interview. Indeed, they were.

*

A couple of the guys were repeat customers but most of them were names Jane didn't recognize. Some of them were called Aaron or Dmitri but most used names like AronZ and Tt445 and Brliner. Sometimes it felt like she was talking to a bunch of gamers and cyborgs, which did make it easier to compartmentalize. This is not real, she'd tell herself as she scrolled through images of Lola in various poses, selecting the perfect merkin shot to send MonsterCming or just the right scat-on-the-face shot to send to Tt445.

One afternoon, Jane was on the floor in the girls' bedroom flipping through books about baby animals. "Foal," she was saying, and, "Look, this baby elephant is picking up a leaf!" At the same time, she was quickly replying to a sext from StarShootsShot, who was telling her about the raging boner he wanted to tap against her neck. That's the type of thing she couldn't wait to tell Curly. Dick taps on necks. Jane imagined Curly saying something like, *Just the tap?*

Yes, yes, yes, they'd respond to almost anything Jane conjured up.

Baby, let's imagine you inside me, she'd type as she sent over an image of Lola inserting a double-sided dildo. With a little prompting, they'd ask to see the video, which featured Lola masturbating the dildo as if it were her own dick, fucking herself to ecstasy. They'd go: *Yes, yes, yes!*

More more more!

And she'd be like, *Cha-chigga-ching-ching!*

It seemed important to some customers to tell Lola that it really hurt. StarShootsShot returned almost daily to chat with Lola, hoping she'd ask if he was okay. *Is it hurting you, sweetie?* Jane would type. *Very much*, he'd write. *Aw hon, let it free*, Jane would write. When men sent pictures of their throbbing, angry dicks, Jane would look away and imagine instead a purple rubber dildo flopping out of their pants. She didn't want to see anyone's dick. But she'd write: *Yes yes yes,* and they'd go, *Yes yes yes yes YES!*

Cha-cha-cha-ching!

During one of those types of moments, on an afternoon where the girls hadn't napped very long, Jane was typing *Ya ya ya ya* and then the front door opened and closed with an efficient little slam. The sound of someone setting heavy bags on the floor and then, "Hi, my sweeties!" from Lorrie. The wall clock was about to choo-choo two times.

"Well you're home early!" Jane called back, hoping her tone didn't sound disappointed. She fumbled to dim her computer screen but not turn it off. The messages kept rolling in, the breathy men were waiting. *Yes? Yes? Yes?* She could feel them typing.

"Dentist appointment," Lorrie said as she walked in, dropped her satchel on the couch, and kneeled by the girls. She kissed the top of each head. "So, how were they? How are you? Doing okay?"

Jane sat up and wiped the metaphorical jizz from her mouth, tilted her head as if to say, *What do you mean?*

"Oh, you just look a little flushed."

"Oh!" Jane said too eagerly. "Yeah, I got this email. A friend… thing." She waved a hand like, *You know how things come up*. She could almost hear the faint ding of messages on her computer, all of those customers left mid-boner. *Yes? Yes? Yes?*

"Oh, dear. Well, I hope everything's okay," Lorrie said, adding with a face that matched: "I know how *that* goes."

Jane nodded like she also knew.

"They ate okay?" Lorrie asked, hardly looking at her nanny as she kneeled next to her girls. She flipped her hair out of her face and looked up at Jane with a squinty smile, as if she had just enough time to hear about it.

Jane made her typical report. How Zooey was picking up whole, cooked green beans with her hands and eating them. How they both pooped, had a good morning nap. "Might be almost time for that post-lunch nap," Jane said, looking at the time on her phone. Which is when Jane noticed she had a text from Lola. She imagined Lola noticing long pauses in activity, asking where she had gone.

But c'mon! Was she not allowed to leave the computer for five minutes?

C'mon, babe! She imagined Lola saying. *The horny peo-*

ple are waiting, sweetie!

"Lorrie?" Jane said to bring herself back into the room. "Has anyone ever told you that you look like Helen Hunt?"

Lorrie nodded like she'd heard it before then kissed the air in the direction of a big-eyed rubber giraffe Zooey was waving in her face, which made Jane think of one of the questions on her sexting application: *A customer is telling you he likes to get slapped in the face with a rubber chicken while he holds a second rubber chicken between his ass cheeks and jerks off. Describe your methods for pleasing this rubber chicken lover.*

Franny leaned over and grabbed the giraffe from her sister and gnawed at its face with her gummy mouth. "Oop, there it goes!" Lorrie laughed. "Into the mouth!"

Inta the mouth. That was the phrase a customer named XXX liked to use. He'd sent a video of himself wearing an enormous strap-on over a pair of khaki shorts and said he wanted Lola to wear one, too. He'd help her fasten it on over a furry, assless suit he would give her, then while she walked around like an ape he'd try to catch her by sticking his finger up her butt. After that routine he'd put his own girthy strap on *inta the mouth*. He and Lola were supposed to writhe around like mating apes while a circle of men stood around watching. During that extended role play, Jane was the best Lola she could be: dainty and flirty and monkey-like, going *Mm yes, oo oo ah ah!*

At some point in this fantasy, the circle of watching men coordinated their jack off efforts and at the same time, they'd spritz the monkey lovers with multicolored jizz that looked like silly string. It would come out in thrilling quantities, and by the end everyone was supposed to be moaning and screaming because XXX and Lola would be sliding all over the floor, dangerously close to the edge of a staircase that would appear at one end of the room. *And any minute, we might slip off*, wrote XXX, enjoying the promise of looming danger. *Inta the mouth*, XXX wrote again, reminding Lola that while they were about to fall down a staircase he was shoving his dildo halfway down her throat. *I can barely breathe*, gasped Lola and he said, *Oo oo ah ah*.

Jane tried to have a normal person expression while Lorrie talked about her tooth ache and headache and whatever other aches. The image of herself in a monkey suit was hard to stop imagining, how she was begging XXX to enter her from behind and give her the ol' reach around. She told him that she loved the feeling of having her own dick.

XXX wrote: *Do you want my dildo or my real penis?*

Surprise me, wrote Lola, and then Jane heard the phrase no nanny wants to hear.

"I figured I'd work from home the rest of the afternoon."

Oh god. "Okay, sounds good!" is what Jane said, wondering if Lorrie would ask why her computer was out. But Lorrie seemed too distracted by the fact that she needed to get back to work. A big writer's conference Lorrie was organizing was only two weeks away and lots of last-minute details needed to happen.

"Did I tell you that one of our keynotes bailed? So now I need to find an agent interested in talking about how to pitch romance novels."

Jane's computer sat inches away, holding the boners of all those men who were waiting to exhale. The clock choo-chooed twice and the girls clapped. Four hours 'til Jane was done nannying, two hours 'til she was done sexting. The babies clapped again and Jane joined. Clappy clappy clappy.

"Everything else okay?" Lorrie asked then.

Could Lorrie see how fast Jane's heart was beating? Did she look too distracted when she twirled a curl? Or angry as she pressed the nail of her index finger repeatedly into the pad of her thumb?

"Going great!" Jane said in what felt like Happy Teacher Voice. "I was just thinking about taking them to the beach."

Lorrie thought that was a wonderful idea! She pointed out all the beach toys that were on the porch, reminded Jane that the stroller was great for jogging, if she wanted. "It handles so great in the sand," she said.

You handle me so great, one guy loved to say.

"Actually, do you mind if I run to the bathroom while you're in here?" Jane put her hand on her stomach as if it ached, like she might be a while. Lorrie made a gesture like, *Of course!* So Jane grabbed her laptop casually, like she was just going to put it away. As she walked down the hall she awakened its screen. Forty-three messages from six different people. *Hi, sweetie!* she wrote to all six of them, then copied and pasted the same thing to each: *Oh my goodness, darling. You got me so excited I started touching myself.*

It felt like the stupidest thing to say. Would Lola ever say such a thing? Would any of her other sexters? Jane brought the laptop into the bathroom and sat on the closed toilet, looking for the perfect Lola pictures to send out.

Then, a flurry of exchanges:

MrDaddio: *What are you up to?* Lola: *Just excited for my plans tonight. ;)*

UserError555: *You make me so hard.* Lola: an emoji of kissy lips and a banana.

GoldyFucks: *Hello? You there?* And then: *I wish I could show you *my* pussy.*

Jane wondered if that last one was from a woman, then she felt like an idiot: of course women were on there. Why not? Maybe some of the dudes—the dirtiest ones—were ladies. Jane wrote back, saying that at the very least *I can show you mine.* GoldyFucks' reply was immediate: *I'm ready.*

Jane flushed the toilet to show she was making progress while GoldyFucks said they were touching themselves for the third time since the conversation began.

Are you coming multiple times? Jane wrote, and without waiting for a reply: *Tell me how.*

GoldyFucks was saying that it's all about who she's with and what she's doing and asked if Lola had seen a film called Peeping Tina? No. *Well let me tell you about it. It's about a lady who is dying from depression. That's how the character phrases it, repeatedly,* GoldyFucks said, adding that the only times the lady feels any joy are the *brief and vibrant moments during masturbation*. The whole film is about this woman getting more and more obsessed with these fleeting moments of pleasure. She tries looking at porn, but that doesn't interest her, so she becomes a people watcher, peering into people's living rooms and bedrooms and kitchens, touching herself while she watches them do mundane things. Dish-washing and dinner-eating, vacuuming and TV-watching. Reading. She starts driving to towns nearby but far enough away from her own town that no one would recognize her if they saw her face peeking in their windows. Finally, GoldyFucks asked: *Do you ever do that?*

Do you? Jane wrote, surprised by her own goosebumps. She flushed the toilet again to make it sound like her time in the bathroom was both progressing and distressing.

She read Lola's text, then: *You're doing great, babe. Not all days are #1!* It was hard to tell if Lola was actually trying to make Jane feel better. Jane did not reply. The messages kept coming.

GoldyFucks: *I just came again.*

UserError555: *I want those kissing lips around my cock.*

Then UserError555 sent a picture of said cock, which reminded Jane of an overstuffed sausage, purplish and bulging out of its casing.

Lola: *Oh my god, yummy yummy! Gimme that!*

MrDaddio: *What're you up to?*

A baby cried in the other room. Lorrie's muffled voice replied. Jane glanced at the time stamp. She'd been in the bathroom for seven minutes.

Lola to GoldyFucks: *Oh yeah? ;) Tell me more so I can, too.*

GoldyFucks: *Because I've been watching you. I guess you could say, I'm a peeper.*

Ew, Jane wanted to write, but she wrote: *Oh yeah?* She included an emoji of dripping water.

Lola to UserError555: *Close your eyes. My lips are there. You feel em baby?*

Lola to MrDaddio: *I'm in the bathroom.*

That one felt like a mistake, but just as Jane was about to correct with **in the shower** she got a reply.

MrDaddio: *Me too. Are you on the toilet?*

Eleven minutes had passed. Jane washed her hands

and sprayed an excessive amount of potpourri to show Lorrie she'd really fucked it up in there. Right before she left the bathroom she responded: *Yes. Are you?*

"Hey, Lorrie, sorry. My stomach has been giving me problems all day," Jane said as she came back into the room. She tried to look pathetic: sad mouth, head tilted, hand on stomach.

Lorrie was a direct communicator. *If you need something, ask for it*, she'd said in their interview. She stood, took off her blazer and said, "I'm sure you saw the antacids in the medicine cabinet?"

"I took three," Jane said in a tone that was accidentally too sad.

"If you're not up for walking, you can always stay here and read with the girls," Lorrie said in a tone that was both motherly and suggested Jane could not go home.

"Oh, I think sunshine will do me good," Jane said, imagining sitting around the house reading to the babies while their mother was just in the other room, coming in and out to get espressos or snacks. She'd make mental notes about Jane's reading style, the way she held the girls, the way she played, talked, joked, laughed. Who could handle that type of surveillance?

Jane gathered organic sun cream and baby bonnets and toys and snacks. When Lorrie wasn't watching, Jane placed her laptop in the basket of the stroller. She hoped her customers could wait a few more minutes, that they'd assume she was too busy masturbating to reply. As she strapped the girls into their stroller, she was thinking words like strap-on and yes and yes and for the first time in those weeks as a sexter, Jane felt like a pervert.

She tried to stop thinking about what she'd say to her customers, the Daddios and the UserErrors, but suddenly it was all she could think about. Peeping Tinas and men in circles, silly jizz spraying like confetti while she linked ape legs with her lover, moaning and yessing and tumbling down the staircase. Her eyes were closing and opening like little windows, she watched herself falling but she wasn't alone. Lola! Lola! They cried. Eyes open, Lola! Don't be shy! Oo oo ah ah!

Lorrie was kissing the girls goodbye, one foot two foot, three foot, four. And Jane, she was saying *Bye! See you soon!* But she could hardly hear anything above all the moaning people, their voices sirening out demands and desires. The babies were cooing from their stroller, babbling along to the portable speakers wedged in the bottom of the basket. It was some *Sparkle Baby* song that sounded like Jingle Bells but that went, *He he he! Hoo hoo hoo! Ha ha ha, ha ha.*

CHAPTER 7

A few days passed. Then came a warm day in June. School was almost out and by afternoon the beaches were already speckled with youth. Teenage girls squealed as they got fake tossed into the ocean. Trucks roared up to the parking lot and soon as their engines were cut, out tumbled groups of strapping young bros carrying boxes of cheap beer and armfuls of hot dogs. Seagulls cawed and swarmed the sky looking for unguarded food; pelicans soared down and grazed their gaping bills into the water. Jane lounged on the deck above it all, watching half-assedly while she answered messages from men who wanted to maintain an imaginary relationship with a woman they thought they knew.

Shortly into that day's exchanges a message popped up from a guy named RandyLocks.

Lola? it started. *I've missed you.*

Hey! I've missed you, too, sweetie! Jane said, curious how long he'd been gone.

I still wanna marry you, baby.

Oh sweetie, Jane started. *How would you handle my late*

night escapades if we were married?

Because, Lola. A long pause between replies, and then: *You already know that I know who you are.*

Jane looked up. A gull had landed on the patio banister and stared empty-brained at the bowl of chips she was eating. Another message dinged.

It turns me on how many men you fuck, insisted Randy-Locks.

Don't forget I fuck women, too.

Oh yeah?

I'd fuck an animal if it paid me enough.

How would you do it?

It went on from there. Back and forth a while until he said something else.

I just love watching you. In your natural habitat.

Jane teased that he'd have to tip harder if he was gonna talk dirty. Immediately a $100 came through so she shrugged and kept talking to him, sassing her other customers by telling them *their* tips weren't as big as *other* guys' tips. A few $20s rolled in, a couple $50s.

I like the way you put your hair behind your ear when you get nervous.

Jane looked at her hands. Had she just put her hair behind her ear? She looked up. The gull flew away. She tried to appear casual as she scanned nearby windows, squinting toward cars parked along the beach. She listened, as if she'd hear footsteps or a door creak, but all that surrounded her were the sounds of waves and laughter and happy screaming; children's voices, music: banda from one direction, pop from another, their styles blending into a bassy mélange that made both songs sound better.

You won't be able to see me, said RandyLocks.

To that, Jane's eyes snapped up. She lowered her baseball cap, pushed her sunglasses harder onto her face. She wanted to type, *What the hell is that supposed to mean?* She pulled up the training manual Lola had sent and searched for a section she'd seen called What to Do When Men Are Being Creepy. After laying out a couple of weak examples, Lola's suggestion was simply to stop replying. It said to check in with Lola before blocking anyone and to not be afraid to ask her what to do if a situation felt uncomfortable.

In the interview, Lola had said: FYI? There's an unsettling number of cops on here. A lot of law enforcement people who have seen too much or *some*-thing. And usually, she added, the most disturbing messages come from those who've worked with criminals or children.

C'mon, love, said RandyLocks. *This isn't a two-way street.*

Jane considered asking what he meant by that, or telling Lola that she had a live one, but her shift was almost over, so she didn't say anything. She just closed the browser and put her computer away. By the time Lorrie and Irene came home, Jane was sitting cross-legged on the floor with their babies, and they were all giggling and laughing about baby things.

*

While Jane fixed them both another tequila sunrise, Curly played with a cigarette, rolling it back and forth between her fingers then dangling it between her lips. She was trying to quit, and part of her tactic was to suck on unlit cigarettes, which seemed like it'd be tempting and unhelpful. Jane had just told her about RandyLocks, which made Curly pace Jane's kitchen, sucking her dry cigarette.

Neither of them said anything for a minute and finally Curly made a face to match: "I think these limes went bad." Then she set her drink aside and said, "Wait, so where'd you end up finishing your sexting shift on the day Lorrie came home early?"

"A bar patio," Jane said. "Oh don't give me *that* look. It's not like I was *drinking*."

"Why didn't you just tell Lola you couldn't finish your shift?"

"I was trying to meet my quota."

"There's a sexting quota?"

"Self-imposed." Jane took a sip of her own drink and agreed that the limes were bad. "I think I made up for my delay with how raunchy I got after, though. I came back on and metaphorically sucked off like ten dudes and this one chick." Jane described the images GoldyFucks had been sending.

"Holy *shit*," said Curly.

"I know."

"Does that get you going?" Curly asked, a little tilt of the head.

"Going?"

"Do you ever?" Curly made an expression to signify her meaning.

"*Oh*. No. Honestly? It just feels like a joke," Jane said, though this wasn't entirely true. In those last few days, it'd been hard to not feel a little flash of sass. Not so much *during* their exchanges—those always felt hurried and businesslike—it was afterwards, when she was driving home and recalling some of the things she'd said, promises and bold actions, all those otherworldly fantasies. Sometimes she would think of those things at night and, you know.

"What happens if Irene and Lorrie find out that you're doing that while their babies are in the room?" Curly sucked on the unlit cigarette, which had become flaccid and moist.

"Can you just light that thing or throw it away?" Jane asked as she led Curly out to the front porch. Something scurried in the brush when they plopped themselves on the top step.

Curly made a big show of finally lighting the cigarette and blew the smoke in Jane's face. She had an expression like, *C'mon, answer my question.* Jane did not answer. And after a few moments of silent smoking Curly asked, "Do you ever see their faces?"

"Not usually. Sometimes, though." Jane tipped back her tequila sunrise, frowned at the bitterness. "One guy wore a ski mask while he fucked a cardboard cutout of me."

"Of Lola," Curly corrected.

"Yeah. Lola."

CHAPTER 8

A few days before the Central Coast Literary Conference, Jane arrived to irritated chatter coming from Lorrie and Irene's kitchen. At first, she assumed it was the stress of the conference. The day before, Lorrie had been frantic when she got home, espresso splashes accentuating her gestures while she paced on the sundeck talking about coordination of vendors and writers and venue.

When Jane made a big auditory show of setting her bag down by the entryway the voices turned to whispers. A hiss of "*You* do it then," was the only part Jane made out.

"Hey there, morning," Irene said. She was wearing a long, silk robe, her wet hair contorted inside one of those terry cloth hair wraps shaped like a seashell. She held a little orange espresso cup in both hands and sipped from it in a way that seemed put on. Franny and Zooey were in their highchairs, picking up pieces of cereal one little O at a time. Regretfully, Jane thought of the customer who jizzed in his Cheerios.

"Morning Zo, morning Fran." Jane took a fat foot from each baby and squeezed it, which made them do a coordinated arm-and-leg flapping trick.

"Jane," Lorrie began with a sigh. She was sitting at the table with the girls and clasped her hands when she looked up. Jane couldn't help but think of Helen Hunt again, and imagined that's who was gesturing for her to please, have a seat.

Jane took the chair next to Zooey, who cooed at her in a coo so sweet it made her want to cry. She said something to that effect and Lorrie made a sound like she agreed. "I love how squishy the tops of their hands are," Jane said as she made an unintentional show of kissing each of Zooey's wiggly fingers.

Lorrie didn't say anything. She was fiddling with the edge of a large, thick envelope, which she patted when she saw Jane looking at it. "NDAs for the literary conference." She patted it again, then pointed at Jane. "Which might be good for you to attend, by the way. They'll have a lot of people talking about publishing. And they're filming both of the keynotes this year. Hence, NDAs," she said again as if she liked the responsibility of the term.

"That sounds great," Jane managed, the back of her brain replaying the hiss of *You do it then*.

"Well, I can get you in for free. I'll put you on the list. You can bring the girls to this Friday's opening."

"That'd be great!" Jane said, thinking, *I don't have a*

choice, do I?

"Some of the speakers are *fabulous*," Lorrie flapped a hand at Jane then pressed it to her heart.

Irene, who'd been standing a few feet from the table, stepped forward then. She dumped back the rest of her espresso and clattered the cup onto its saucer. She set it on the edge of the table and said, "Hey, Love?" then glanced between the choo-choo clock and Lorrie with an expression like, *Let's-get-on-with-it.* Irene had been leaving early most mornings to work on her latest manuscript in an office she rented in Morro Bay. She said the thirty-minute drive up the coast was what she needed to clear her head and get in the mindset. *To write shitty mystery novels?* Jane thought when she heard the routine.

"Jane." Lorrie unclasped her hands then. She put a tuft of shiny blonde hair behind her ear, but the hair immediately fell forward again, too shiny to be held back by something so simple as an ear. Still, Lorrie pushed the tuft back again.

Jane waited for the other tuft to fall. She thought of Lola in their interview, how she put her hair up into a ponytail then took it out again, her fingers constantly moving through that cascading golden hair. Though Curly always insisted on having curl pride, Jane couldn't help but wonder what it'd be like to have straight hair. What it'd be like to be like Lola. She caught herself smiling, and tried to look less dreamy as she put a clump of curls behind her own ear. The frizzy strands clung to each other, just waiting for the chance to be dreaded together forever.

There was a long pause in which she realized she should say something, or that one of the moms was about to say something. *Something*. Something? Jane looked from one face to the other. One silent second passed, then two, and by the third, she was feeling the blood draining from her face. It felt increasingly visceral, like it was being removed via syringe, and she could feel the cold needles pressing into her skin and sucking. Finally, Jane said in a voice that was supposed to sound relaxed: "Yeah?"

"Lorrie and I want to talk to you about something," Irene started. She took off her hair wrap, shook her sharp moist hair around.

"Get the fuck out of our house," Jane imagined them saying. To which she'd go, Well, *technically*? I *am* a sex offender. She was supposed to have gone around telling people. The neighbors, employers. Jane wasn't supposed to be working with kids at all. She forgot what would happen if she didn't disclose that information. Jail time? Eternal shunning?

"We've noticed that you spend a lot of time on your computer while you're with the girls." Irene crossed her arms, tilted her head. Jane imagined Irene was the type of woman who'd taken classes about negotiation, who'd know how to respond when a person said X or Y: she'd hit 'em with a Z.

Jane tried to keep her eyes moving casually between Lorrie and Irene, forcing herself not to scan the house for nanny cams. But of *course* they'd have nanny cams. Who would let a stranger into their home and *not* record them? And maybe they knew about Jane's history after all; maybe they knew but they didn't care, because they understood. Perhaps they, too, would have kissed their boss. They, too, would have been overcome by the moment of porn-induced passion, unzipping and crawling down, mouths open and eyes closed.

Lorrie and Irene's expressions were difficult to decipher but Jane hoped they said: *Everyone deserves a second shot. Misunderstandings happen. You're not a criminal. You're not a slutty creep.*

"Our neighbor let us know about the computer stuff," Irene started, uncrossing her arms to raise her hands in innocence. "I swear we are not spying on you."

"And we do want you to feel relaxed," Lorrie added.

"Our casa."

"Su casa."

"Computer stuff?" Jane tried to sound innocent but her voice was pitchy and nervous.

"Todd mentioned he'd noticed," said Lorrie.

"Todd?" Jane couldn't help it, then. She looked around the room. Who the fuck is *Todd*? She almost said it aloud. She imagined going, *Men can watch me on my time. MY time.* She'd stand and point a thumb to her chest, the same thumb she'd metaphorically stuck repeatedly up her butt.

"Todd Fard," said Lorrie.

"Todd *Fard*?"

"Pretty miserable name, huh?" Irene agreed. "Well anyhow, he said he just happened to notice."

Jane looked around again. "But—what do you mean he just, *noticed*?"

"That he *happens* to notice you're on your computer a lot," Irene said, tightening her robe.

"We *know* you're doing a good job with the girls, from what we can tell," Lorrie said, taking the nearest fat hand and squeezing it.

"And yeah," Irene interjected. "We want this to be a long-term possibility. For all of us."

Lorrie and Irene must have seen the wheels in Jane's head spinning.

"It's what happens when you have a house with a lot of windows." Lorrie shrugged.

The three of them took the moment's lull to wander their eyes out the windows and toward all the other nearby windows. Windows like mirrors, windows like doorways.

"*We* don't mind it," Irene added with her own quick shrug. "Nothin' to hide."

"Me neither," Jane said. And it came so easily, it felt real when she said, "My writing," hand to chest like she was just overcome by the thrill of uttering that word. "I've just been on *such* a roll lately."

Irene? She beamed. Lorrie? She smiled.

Jane, eyes innocent and kind and excited, she didn't just beam or smile. She glowed.

CHAPTER 9

Todd Fard, Jane would learn that night, was a computer engineer who lived next door and apparently had a lot of free time on his hands during the day.

"It's a violation!" Jane was saying, pacing and slamming around her house. She'd canceled that afternoon's sexting routine, afraid of what Todd Fard might be seeing.

"How do you think he's watching?" Curly asked, furiously sucking the tip of an unlit cigarette. Jane had one, too, and they were both pacing around like that, tripping over things in Jane's messy house. Books and mail and shoes and jackets, *Who cares, I'm gonna move soon*, she kept telling Curly as they kicked all her stuff out of the way or trampled it. There was something satisfying about stomping on your own things. "Binoculars?" Curly tried.

They stopped mid-pace. Two sets of shudders as they imagined the same thing: a pair of eyes, watery from their exhaustive focus; a mouth parted just enough to dismiss waves of heaty, dank breath; skin ill from diminished sun exposure, less and less of it as they watched the world from inside, glued to windows, glued to screens. A Peeping Todd. The hands, fat in a not-cute way, gripped greedy binoculars.

"Or a telescope," Jane suggested, imagining a single eye zooming in on her computer screen. Todd Fard was watching the men shitting their pants then using their own feces as lubricant, he was watching their strap-ons and Cheerio jizz. And there was Jane, the Great Lola Impersonator, responding with pictures of a beautiful, tan-stomached woman humping the corner of her bed, a neon green dildo up her butt. She's going yahoo! while she shotguns Mountain Dew and howls with such believable pleasure she should win an Oscar, while all the RandyLocks of the internet shat and masturbated in her honor.

That's when Jane paused. Curly paused.

"Do you think Todd Fard is RandyLocks?" Jane whispered.

They debated the possibility, wondering if he was the type of computer engineer who knew how to hack. If he was on Lorrie and Irene's network and could somehow tap into the activity of Jane's screen, he was infiltrating her world by way of randy pseudonym. Curly and Jane were picturing the hacker from *Jurassic Park* then, the same actor who played Newman on Seinfeld. He'd been typecast as an evil, gross guy. Maybe Todd Fard was greasy and large, too. Maybe he was wedged into his computer chair watching as Jane engaged in men's raunchiest fantasies. The number of times she'd jacked off a centaur or a sphinx; the scat she'd had to sift through; the way she'd shrunk down to the size of a Barbie doll and climbed inside that one guy's butt, feet-first so her head was the only thing sticking out, she'd kneaded her little feet into his prostate and screamed. It's the only way I can finish, he'd told Jane, and she'd shrugged and pounded her Barbie feet, watching the commissions roll in.

"By the way." Curly sucked at the dry tobacco. "How are they not more disturbed by this neighbor watching their kids?"

"Are they not strong independent women?" Jane agreed, hands raised in a what-the-fuck?

"Or maybe they *asked* him to keep an eye. Make sure you were doing a good job."

Jane glanced toward her own windows then, all of which were curtained, locked. She didn't want any Todd Fards or Peeping Tinas.

"Wait, so how'd it end with Lorrie and Irene?"

"I told them I was working on a short story. They seemed to like that." Jane made a gesture like a lighter. "C'mon, Curls, don't look at me like that."

"So are you gonna quit?"

"Smoking?"

"Your job." Curly flung her cigarette into the trash with flair.

"Which one?"

Curly looked at Jane like she *must* not be serious. "The *sexting* one."

Jane confessed that the sexting one, though very part time, paid even more than the nanny one. That with this kinda money, she could finally move out of her childhood home, she could do something.

"Like what?" Curly asked.

"Anything!" Jane said.

"So how much are you actually making?"

"Between both jobs?" Jane made a gesture like she was counting, thinking. "Six figures."

"What!"

With a shrug and a fake smudging out of her unlit cigarette, Jane was like, "Sex sells, baby."

CHAPTER 10

The next day, Jane asked the girls if they'd ever made a fort. In response they cooed and sucked their hands and threw wooden fruit. Jane narrated her fort building process for their amusement.

"Okay, first we need a chair," she said, pointing at their vocabulary word. "Chair." She continued until she had four chairs, a king-sized sheet, and a toy that projected stars onto the ceiling. When she clicked ON the girls made noises like "oOooOOoo" and crawled in. Before entering the fort herself, Jane paced the bedroom, looking out the floor-to-ceiling windows at the ocean below, the post-lunch beach walkers, the gulls. The windows of neighboring houses reflected the oceanic scene, the bright blueness of sky. It was difficult to imagine which windows belonged to Todd Fard: the concrete house? The wooden one? The stucco?

Jane crawled inside the fort, set each baby up with a picture book about animals then fired off her first few messages. One guy was ready to get right into it, showing her a picture of his hideous little wiener, which he referred to as his Camaro. Jane told him that it was the perfect size for her garage, which is really tight on space but has just enough room for his sweet lil' engine machine. Camaro dick roared with delight. Another guy wanted to talk about his day, going on and on about his wife and kids, how miserable he was. What's it all mean and et cetera. Per Lola's suggestion, Jane was gentle about her replies until the twenty minute mark, at which point she asked him for tips, hoping the reminder of her role in his world wouldn't send him over the edge he kept referencing.

A repeat customer named UrbanSowboy was, once again, humping a plastic pig. *Yee haw, baby*, is how Jane chimed in on the exchange, imagining her voice all country-like. *You sure know how to wrangle 'em, honey*, she added, because she knew UrbanSowboy was not interested in hearing about Lola. He just wanted praise and the occasional video of Lola *yankin her turkey,* as he called it. It seemed to make him feel very manly to tip well. Sometimes he'd send her fifty or a hundred bucks at the end and tell Lola to take herself to a nice dinner, pretend they were on a date.

Well ain't you sweet.

That morning, UrbanSowboy sent a short video of himself slapping that pig's little plastic butt. When Jane typed, *Oh my lord! Ride that hog, honey!* He went faster and faster and at the end he looked right into the camera, so Jane sent over a picture of Lola tipping a cowboy hat in approval. *Yee-haw, baby.*

Cha-ching!

And then a new message came in.

You're a funny bunny, said RandyLocks.

And immediately, there it was again: that sensation like needles. They poised, grazed her jawline, her cheeks, her neck, waiting and waiting and waiting and when he said, *Do you think people don't know about you?* the sharp points penetrated and sucked, they drained Jane's color and heat and she had to lie down on the pillows and blankets on the floor. Two sets of fat hands patted her back, touched her cold face, pressed into her cheeks and presented her with wooden fruit. In Jane's worry she still had the mindset to pick up a banana, call for help.

"Hello?" Jane said, handing the wooden fruit to Zooey, who made a noise into it, recognizing they were pretending it was a phone again.

Don't think they don't know, he added.

Know what? Jane typed but didn't send. She tried, *What're you talking about, silly billy?* but deleted that, too. *Who is this?* Delete. Jane remembered Lola telling her how many cops were on there, lots of stressed-out policemen with a brand of fury that needed a certain kind of comfort.

Are you fucking with me? Jane typed. Stared. Sent. Waited. She lay on her back, looking up into the fake stars. They spun above her while the babies patted her body with their fat little hands.

Yes I am.
Pat pat pat.

*

Jane lay on the floor next to her bed that night, surrounded by piles of clothes and shoes, her old quilt halfway draping off the bed and covering part of her legs. Something scurried by a window and Jane imagined it was outside but still, she sat up and looked around the room for rodents or Fards.

Do you think Todd Fard can actually see me? she texted Curly.

Right now?

Jane shuddered and wrote: *Well, I meant at work…*

I dunno know, dude.

Jane imagined Todd Fard had found a way to connect to every device in their house. He could be watching Jane through the computer, listening through the baby monitors, watching through those old school security cameras. She had tried to figure out which home was his and finally decided it must be the wooden one next door. *Because*, she'd reasoned to Curly, *wifi signals probably go through wood easiest.*

And, it's right next door, Curly agreed.

Todd Fard is totally RandyLocks, huh? Jane waited for Curly to reply. A few minutes went by, an hour. Then Jane had a fairly unreasonable thought: *Has Todd Fard infiltrated our texts?*

Finally, Curly replied: *I think you need to quit that sexter job, dude. It's fucking with your head.*

But the money. I could finally move out of this shit hole.

You can move out of that shit hole without the money, too.

Psh! To what, something equally shitty?

Jane was walking around her house, then, stepping around things or stomping across them. If Todd Fard came for her, at least she'd hear him coming. He'd trip on a tupperware container, pop some bubble wrap, step on a squeaky toy for the dog she no longer had. Jane pressed packing tape along the perimeter of each window in the house, so when he forced them to open at least she'd hear the untaping, a sound that was unmistakably that of paint peeling off wall. Before swishing each curtain closed, she peered into the darkness that was cement and weeds and rodents. What would it be like to go to bed each night to the sound of waves crashing? Just outside, you could picture it: the tide rising, falling.

CHAPTER 11

The Central Coast Literary Conference was held at a convention center in San Luis Obispo. Before Jane undid the girls from their carseats, she sent a quick text to Lola. *Just a reminder, I had to take the day off!*

No reply.

She got out of the family's luxury SUV, pushed a button and waited for the trunk to slowly rise. Dozens of people herded past her toward two sets of double doors. It was an interesting mélange of folks that all gave off the same vibe—she'd heard about all this—and there they were in real life: the book nerds and mentor-seekers, writers-to-be, people desperately looking for guidance on books they didn't know how to write. There were people who'd saved up a lot of hard-earned money to be there, the ones who'd get up before their awful day jobs and write first thing in the morning. There were bus drivers who shared stories about writing before dawn; parents whose only quiet time was after midnight. Then there were the people who could pay anything to get their book published. They'd hire editors and ghostwriters, pay off the right agents to take them on. Their books would appear by grocery check out lines, rounded letters on bright covers with gleaming photos of the author, the ghostwriters and editors quietly acknowledged in the back with the same nod of a thank-you they gave to the family dog. And their books would sell, because they could afford the marketing teams, the ones who'd pay premiums to save a spot at the front table displays of all the bookstores. The VIP table of books. Those were the ones real writers resented. When Jane gave that spiel, Curly ripped off the tip of her cigarette and tilted her head with an expression like a question. Jack told me that, Jane said. He actually *was* writing a book. About what? Curly asked. Jane made a face like, I dunno. You didn't ask? No.

"What are *you* most excited for?" the lady in the car next to Jane asked.

"I really don't know," Jane sighed, double checking that each baby was secure in her stroller seat. She jiggled the straps, which made the girls giggle. "Entertainment, I hope?"

Silence. Jane looked up to realize the woman was talking to someone else, a lady with blue hair and a t-shirt that said Books Are My Lovers. Rather than say anything, the ladies looked at each other with faces like, *Uhm?* So Jane raised her eyebrows back in one that said, *Okay?*

"Loosen up, Jane," she said to herself like she was talking to the girls.

Jane strolled the double-wide through the entryway, which was decorated with images of authors in varying degrees of acclaim: a woman who wrote a memoir about hitchhiking through the South; a so-called financial guru; a bright-cheeked children's book author holding up his very successful book about a slug. The girls clapped as they passed under an archway made of balloons. After another archway Jane read aloud a banner that proclaimed, "Welcome to the Book Shoppe!" Spelled with an extra E like that, as if it were so quaint. Tables of books lining the perimeter of a convention center ballroom hardly felt like a "shoppe" but at least they knew their audience.

Books Are My Lovers.

The babies sat patiently in their stroller while Jane stopped and picked up books, flipping them over to glance at their backs for no reason other than killing time. They meandered by tables lined with books that might as well have been called *Regurgitated White People Buddhism* and *Rich People Problems*. In the romance section were titles like *Surprise Surprise!* and *My Sweet Helper*, which sounded just as saccharine and mommy-centered as the children's book titles.

Irene's books were there, too, of course. A big display of her mystery novels took over half a table. Jane thought of the phrase *It's all about who you know.*

"Look, it's Momma's books!" Jane pointed. Franny propped her feet on the stroller handrail. Zooey stuck a foot in her mouth. Jane picked up a paperback called *The Lady's Caper* and another called simply, *The Caper*. Both covers were dark red and featured a cloaked figure, a magnifying glass, a globe. "Irene Finnley is a writer living in Central California. She has published thirty-two books to date," Jane read to Franny and Zooey. "Look! You see Momma?" She pointed to Irene's picture, in which she is leaning against what appears to be a library shelf. Her arms are crossed and she is wearing an unflattering gray turtleneck that makes her look like a '90s sitcom divorcée. Franny and Zooey were unimpressed, too distracted by the crowds and their own feet. They moved on until something else caught Jane's eye.

At the far end of the Shoppe were stacks of hardcover books arranged in an octagonal shape at the feet of a life-size cardboard cutout. Jane strollered through the hum of the crowd, drawn to the cutout as much as everyone else was. The banner read: *Noon! Keynote lunchtime with Lola. Come see one of America's favorite porn stars read from her new memoir,* Sexy Life, Hello.

Jane looked at the stack of pink books. She picked one up. *Sexy Life, Hello*, it cooed. On the front was the Lola that Jane had become so familiar with: her buoyant breasts, her tanning-boothed skin, her plush lips that were parted in a way meant to say: I'm seductive, I'm fun, I'm friendly.

"Hey there! You made it." Lorrie was gliding over with the air of someone confidently in charge. A walkie-talkie was clipped to her pants; her eyes were alert, scanning the room for anything that needed improving. Satisfied, briefly, in what she saw, Lorrie kneeled in front of the double-wide, kissed two sets of chubby feet.

"You know her?" Jane held out Lola's book, shook it a little toward Lorrie.

"Oh, *sure*. I mean, not personally, but I know her publicist, obviously, and her assistant." Lorrie stood, arms crossed, head tilted. She admired the cut-out as if she'd made it herself. "She's a *doll*, really."

They admired the image: Lola in cut-off jean shorts, the white fringe hanging several inches down her thighs. The button fly, undone and folded over, hints at the top of her Brazilianed pudenda. Her bright pink tank top can barely contain her breasts, which she is not shy in admitting are fake. I mean, *obviously*, she'd famously said in an interview with a cock-eyed television host.

"She seems cool," Jane agreed while the Rolodex of images flipped through her mind: Lola humping a plastic sheep, Lola with chocolate all over her stomach, Lola screeching as an unknown hand eases a dildo called The LeBron up her hooha.

"Well, I'd say you should come watch the keynote but you'd need a lunch ticket and it's sold out. Actually— hold on. Jon?" Lorrie was calling to someone in her walkie-talkie, then pointing it antennae-first toward a passing crew member. "Kaylee, are the Pitch-a-Thon sign-up stations all working?"

The blonde head nodded as it breezed past, calling over the shoulder, "Tablets are working brilliantly!"

"Thanks, Kaylee!"

A hand raised in reply.

Lorrie nodded once, a contented expression, walkie at the ready. Jane admired a person so in their element. What did that feel like? Lorrie cheeped again into her walkie: "Jon, can you confirm if there is one seat? I have an attendee here with a stroller." Without waiting for a reply she added. "Let's go ahead and set up a handicap spot near the front?"

Jane flapped a hand, mouthed, *The back!* then gestured at the girls, the doorway, made a face like, *In case they need to be changed.* She looked for the convention center exit, scanned the crowd while a feeling she couldn't name reverberated along her limbs, settled in her chest. And then she recognized the sensation. The needles, the cold. It was dread that had come for her, it reached through her skin and grabbed tight to her stomach, the organ itself was pulsing in a fist.

Lorrie was saying something and Jane wasn't listening, she was watching the multitudes: the shiny foreheads and slicked hair, the backpacks and totes slung over shoulders, the hopeful expressions, the nerded-out joy. Expectations. And she found herself scanning the crowd for eyes looking more than hopeful; eyes that were expectant and serious. Intent and Fard-like. Randy-like and StarShootsShot-like.

"So many people came to see her," Lorrie was saying, "That we decided to livestream it, too."

"Oh." She didn't mean to say it like that. Like, Oh *no*. DonaldMuck and MonsterCming, AronZ, Tt445, Brliner. None of them seemed real until she saw the flock of men flooding through the doors into the dining hall, taking their seats to see the great Lola in real life, in bones and flesh. A balding, sweaty man wearing a dinosaur T-shirt walked by, and from the back, Jane saw that he was wearing a small green children's backpack in the shape of Yoshi from *Super Mario Bros*. She wondered if he liked centaurs and pigs. His thumbs were looped through his little backpack straps and Jane imagined them being shoved up his butt, up her butt, up Lola's butt. Everyone's thumb was up a butt. And then a stupid thought came to her, she couldn't shake it *despite* how stupid: would they recognize *her* somehow?

"Jane?"

Jane nodded but she didn't know why. Two sets of chubby legs started kicking in cheery unison, begging for attention.

"So you want to feed them in here, then?" Lorrie was looking at her with raised eyebrows like, *Earth to Jane*.

"Mhmm, mhmm," Jane mustered. "Sorry, just so—*exciting* in here." She felt like she might just shit her pants.

What if she did? Would that be a good excuse to leave? Or just get fired.

"Oh, it's my favorite day of the year. Hi, sweet girl," Lorrie cooed to Franny, who was sitting up and tugging at her mother's cardigan. Then to Zooey, who was flailing a foot around until Lorrie caught it, gave it a squeeze. "Hi, my girls." Kiss kiss kiss.

Jane was never sure how to be in moments like that. It made her think of watching two people kiss, it's sweet but you give it privacy, you look away. So, she looked at Lola's cutout, the way the tip of her tongue touched the side of her lips. Everyone who passed it looked up and down. How could they not? It wasn't even just the men. Kids and moms, young women and old. She was mesmerizing. Somehow both sexual and motherly, overpowering yet friendly. Welcoming, warm, wanting.

The walkie cheeps made Jane start, so she put a hand to her mouth, like she'd burped instead of flinched.

"No problem, Lorrie."

"Jon, actually toward the back, by an exit door."

"You got it."

"Okay, guys, 'bout half an hour 'til you should get in there and take your seat. Peruse the bookstore! Feel free to put a couple kids' books on my card for the girls," Lorrie said, absentmindedly handing Jane her credit card as she looked over her shoulder, nodding toward a staff member who must have been gesturing about something that needed confirmation.

"Okay," Jane said like a robot, scanning the atmosphere for all the Randys and Fards. She thought of a new plan: buy the kids' book about the slug, then leave. No more Randys. Get away from the Fards. And it was in *that* moment, Jane realized she would quit the Lola job. No amount of money was worth that level of daily stress. So, she conjured a quick and reasonable three-part plan: leave conference, write an I-quit email, ponder life's existence.

"*There* she is!" Lorrie raised her hands above her head in a gesture more excited than Jane had ever seen her make. She draped her arms over Irene, who'd just come over with flushed cheeks and a glowing smile. "How'd it go, Love?"

"It went great. It really did." Irene leaned her head on Lorrie's shoulder with an expression that said: *This is the stuff of life*. In recognizing that expression's meaning, Jane felt an incredible sadness for her own existence and she wondered: *What is the stuff of* my *life?*

Lorrie's walkie cheeps started cheeping and Jane was having this feeling like, *Fuuuuck.*

"Jon, sorry can you add a second chair to that handicap spot?"

"Got it!"

The moms smiled and squeezed their baby's feet and smiled at Jane, too, like they were all about to have such a nice lunch. Like, this was just such a nice day. Nice nice

nice.

"Can you hold the stroller for two minutes while I use the bathroom?" Jane asked, feeling strange to ask if the kids' mothers minded watching her own kids.

"Sure, sure," they said.

Jane moved through the crowd, where every man could be a Fard. She imagined him stopping her, grabbing her elbow in that annoying way people do when they know you don't really want to talk to them. She couldn't imagine what came beyond the elbow grab. Maybe nothing. Maybe Todd Fard would haunt her with his presence, he'd keep watching, saying little of importance. He just wanted Jane to know he was watching. That was his thrill. The peeping.

"Jane?" said a familiar voice. A voice she had wanted to hear for so long. But in that moment, the voice sounded startling and judgemental and worrisome. "Are you okay?" Jack almost touched her arm but then he looked over her shoulder as if… someone else was there.

Jane whipped around to confirm that no one else was there. No one was watching her that she could see, but that didn't mean they weren't watching.

Jack titled his head as if to say: *What is going on with you?* To confirm this expression, he said, "What's going on?"

"With me?"

Jack laughed. Nervously, it seemed.

Why didn't you write me back? Jane wanted to ask, but instead she pointed at the blue folder under his arm. The kind that kids put in their three-ring binders to hold dittos and homework. "What are you doing here?" she asked.

He held out the blue folder. She opened it.

"The Sound of a Laugh," Jane read aloud. "What is this? This your book?"

"It's a query letter, yeah. I'm pitching it. I have a two o'clock appointment at the Pitch-a-Thon." With a nervous smile Jack explained the process of reading his one-pager aloud, of trying to sell an agent on his book idea.

"They actually publish books at this thing?"

"Well, some agents take on clients, or at least ask for their manuscript. Then if they *like* it, they might sign you and pitch you to publishers. I've lost you."

"No you haven't," Jane said. Too earnestly. "I just thought, that guy—" she pointed at a dude with a pointy waxed goatee in a *Finding Neverland* T-shirt—"that he was someone. Nevermind." *You look healthy*, she wanted to say, but she knew if she said it her voice would sound too surprised—his gut was slimmed, his skin shone, somehow he looked less bald—so she started with, "So."

"So," Jack said.

He took the folder back. Put it back under his arm.

Jane was waiting for the part where he would tell her that his life was over and crushed because of her. That he missed her and hated her, but that also he longed for her, thought about her *all* the time. Maybe if he said that, she could ask how he'd been doing. Maybe she'd apologize, could take a little credit for ruining his life. *Did I ruin your life?* she almost asked. She tried to put on an expression that said: *What about us?* But Jack spoke first.

"What about you?" he said.

"Me?" What did that mean? She didn't know, and said simply, "I'm working here."

"Oh, wow! For the Literary Conference?" Jack asked, and without waiting for her to confirm, he looked at his watch. "Well, I guess I'll head into the keynote. Everyone *loves* her, but I think she's a hack. Do you know she has like a dozen people that sext for her? She has this whole online fan world, with all these impersonators sexting for her at all hours."

"Hah. Uh-huh," Jane said like an idiot, wondering: *Wait, how many me's are in here?* Were the Randys and Fards aware of all the impersonators? Is that how the world thought of them? Impersonators?

"Eh, sex sells." Jack shrugged.

Who was watching who? Or *whom*? Whom was watching whom? And as Jack was asking what she did for the conference, a cheer made its way through the crowd like a wave.

"Oh *god*, speak of the devil," he said.

On the other side of the shoppe the multitudes

were parting, they were cheering and murmuring and open-mouthedly watching as Lola was escorted by two bulky security guards wearing matching pink polos. Her silky white gown hovered just above the floor and boasted a slit that snaked so far up her thigh it was almost in hip territory. Her hair was tied up in the shape of a bow.

"All-American sweetheart," Jack said, commenting on the publicity stunt of her crowd work, how she walked very slowly, smiled broadly, her pink-nailed hand raised above heads and waving queen-like to the people. Phones were in the air, flash flash, snap snap.

"Jack? Do you ever think about that day? With Liza?" Jane asked over the crowd.

"What?" he shouted then because it was so loud all of a sudden, the crowd was just brimming with voices. Then, Jack wasn't looking at Jane anymore. No one was. She scanned the crowd and located her bosses, their babies: they were on the far side of the room, at the corner near the Lola cutout. Lorrie and Irene were each holding a baby, and both babies were waving their chubby hands to anyone who would wave back.

"Jack!" Jane shouted again.

"What?"

Lola's entourage was getting closer.

"Liza Spinelli!" Jane shouted.

"WHAT ABOUT IT?"

"THAT DAY!"

Then Jane could see her, getting closer and closer. It was Lola, in real life. Only a few feet away. The real life Lola.

Wow.

Lola was hugging a gray-haired woman in an old Shania Twain T-shirt that was just long enough to cover her big, flat butt.

"BEST DAY OF MY LIFE!" Jack shouted.

"REALLY?" Jane's eyes were still on Lola but she stepped sideways, closer to Jack. She thought about taking his hand.

"DEFINITELY!"

Jane's heart fluttered with I knew it, I *knew* it! Her hand tingled like she was really going to do it, she'd reach over and link her fingers between his. Or she'd turn to him, she'd take his face in her hands and kiss his lips and close her eyes and they'd let the crowd swarm around them, the entourage would pass and nothing of anything else would matter. Make that two, she thought. Two I-quit emails. She no longer wanted any of what she was doing. But then her fingers curled in like a dying spider when he clarified:

"GOT ME THE FUCK OUT OF THAT PLACE." He held up the blue folder. Kissed it. And in a quieter voice but one that she could still hear, he said, "I'm finally doing what I want."

And then came a squeal.

"Oh my *god*!" Lola was saying, waving in their direction. "Janey!" Lola cried, taking very fast but very shallow steps toward Jane, who watched the quick little feet in their bedazzled high top sneakers as they got closer, closer. Lola's hands and arms extended and the crowd in front of her parted like an ambulance was coming through. Then Lola cried, "Sweetie!"

Jack stepped back and Jane almost did, too, but she knew that somehow (somehow!) that greeting was for her. Then Lola was wrapping her arms around Jane's neck, then leaning back, one hand on each of Jane's shoulders. "My *God*," Lola said, smiling and giggling. She pressed her forehead against Jane's forehead and said, "*You*, my sweetie, are my biggest star."

Jane felt the heat in her face and a shyness she forgot she possessed came over her, then. She couldn't think of anything to say. The gray-haired woman in the Shania Twain t-shirt was waving at her, at Lola. Lola stood next to Jane then, one arm draped around Jane's shoulders like a shawl.

"That's Charlotte," Lola said in Jane's ear. "She's got the shift right after yours."

"That don't impress me much," Jane said. Lola laughed but it was clear she had no idea why Jane had said that. Jane pointed at the caption on Charlotte's Shania Twain shirt.

Lola was smiling, waving, saying, "Isn't this *fun*?"

"Well," Jane started, her eyes darting toward Jack, whose mouth hung down to his sweet, sweet belly. "I mean, aren't you afraid of people knowing?"

"WHAT?" Lola had to shout then because the crowd was closing in around them. Phones were out in a swarm of amateur paparazzi. Snap snap, flash flash. "KNOW WHAT?" Lola's arm was slung over Jane's shoulder. Lola was basking in the photos like sunshine. Some people were filming. Live streaming. Then a boom mic was hovering over the crowd, right over Jane and Lola's heads. Jane looked into the camera, thinking: NDA.

"I mean, about me and stuff," Jane fumbled.

"WHAT, BABY?" Lola was shouting to Jane but she was looking into the crowd, her tanned leg reaching out from the slit in her dress like a come-hither finger. And her arm, it was still around Jane, of all people. Jane, a woman in jeans and a tank top with a blueberry stain near the navel.

"About me," Jane repeated, smiling briefly at Charlotte to acknowledge her hand, which was still waving at her. "And Charlotte. And all the others. I mean, aren't you afraid of people knowing it's not you?"

"Afraid?" Flash flash, snap snap. Lola leaned close to Jane's ear, so close Jane thought she'd give it a nibble. Jack was watching, locking eyes with Jane's, tilting his head like, *Wait, what?* Flash flash, snap snap. Lorrie and Irene were still standing at the base of Lola's cutout, their heads tilted with expressions like, *What in the actual hell?* The boom mic was so close that Jane could almost feel its furry cover as it inched closer to their mouths. And that's when Lola looked at Jane, her eyes twinkling and her mouth cocked in playful smirk. She took Jane's face in one hand, smushing her cheeks a little as she leaned in and kissed her with parted lips. Her breath was soft and warm and she said, "Sweetie? I'm not afraid of nothin'."

ACKNOWLEDGEMENTS

Thank you, always, to my dearest friend Bronwyn Howlett Peterson, for never once doubting any of my wild n crazy guy ideas. Love you, sis. Thank you to the Trinity for your unwavering confidence and support. Elizabeth Butter Mercury, Brenna Uni Nelson, I love you as Prince loves you. Jesse Bo Widmark, thank you for *getting* me and for reminding me that my voice is unique, and that my work and myself deserve to exist. Thanks to Jarrod Ackerley for talking about stories with me for so many hours and for always having such great questions and insights. Thank you Kiki Cake of Soap, for hearing me and seeing me and giving me so much space to talk about my writing with you. Thanks to any friend I've ever had who let me blather on about writing.

Thanks to my parents, James and Sharon Kicherer, for your love and for telling me you're proud of me... but also for not asking what this book is about (sorry, guys, you probably shouldn't read this). My brothers, Adam and David, for always making me feel cool and for cracking up when you read my stuff. That's all the motivation

I need sometimes.

Thank you oh so much to my San Francisco writing group for all your feedback and support over the years. Audrey Tran, Catherine Bator, Scott Morrison and especially to Fred Campagnoli. Fred, you were one of the first people to really "get" my writing and make me feel like I could actually make someone laugh through the written word. I'm still trying to figure out "Funicular Situation."

Thank you to Ryan Johnson for your incredible illustration, I love this cover so much! Thank you Gwendolyn Schulte at GRS Editorial for your edits and layout work. Thank you Brenna Chase for drawing the original Banana Pitch illustration on a napkin at The Night Light in Oakland (RIP). It means so much to me that someone would spend any amount of their time on my work.

Thank you to the small presses who long listed this novella and the ones who made offers on it. Thank you to the Regional Arts and Cultural Council for the grant that made the *Sexy Life, Hello* audiobook production possible. That grant also inspired the print run of this novella, as well as the launching of Banana Pitch Press. Excited to bring other writers' work into the world, too.

Thank you reader, for reading. I am so honored you just spent two or three hours of your life with this wacky book.

And of course, thank you Pancake and Belly, for sitting at my feet for hours and hours while I write. If only any of us could be as sweet and pure as a dog.

www.ingramcontent.com/pod-product-compliance
Lightning Source LLC
Chambersburg PA
CBHW030819070225
21556CB00004B/38